IN THE COMPANY
OF WOLVES

IN THE COMPANY OF WOLVES

STEVE LANG

In The Company of Wolves

Copyright © 2017. 2025. Steve Lang.

For permission requests, write to the publisher, addressed "Attention: Permissions Coordinator," at the address below.

ISBN: 979-8-9899782-6-7 (Paperback)
ISBN: 979-8-9899782-5-0 (Hardcover)
ISBN: 979-8-9899782-7-4 (Digital/Kindle)
ISBN: 979-8-9899782-8-1 (Audio)
ISBN: 979-8-9899782-9-8 (Hardback/Barnes & Noble)

Cover design by Gonzalo Rodriguez
Interior layout by Mirko Fermani
Printed in the United States of America.

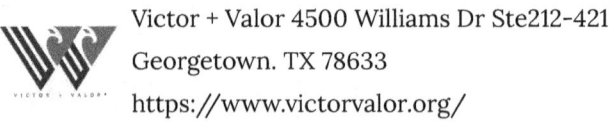

Victor + Valor 4500 Williams Dr Ste212-421
Georgetown. TX 78633
https://www.victorvalor.org/

More information about the author can be found at https://stevedlang.com

First Printing: 2017

For Nicholas, with all my love

ACKNOWLEDGMENTS

Special thanks to David Wilcock, Graham Hancock, Richard Hoagland, Dr. Steven Greer for the Disclosure Project, and Joseph Campbell for his The Hero with a Thousand Faces.

I'd also like to thank my editor, Charlie Michener and William Wood for a fantastic cover.

TABLE OF CONTENTS

CHAPTER 1

IT WAS A DARK SUMMER night in the year 2060. Cold, hard rain pounded the three-hundred-acre cattle ranch Derrick "Mac" MacDonald and his family-owned. They were waiting out the latest in a series of torrential downpours as hail pelted their roof and windows like BB's from the sky. Their single-story ranch house shook and bumped with each clap of thunder from the tormented sky while lightning bolts illuminated the soggy air. Mac worriedly rubbed his five o'clock shadow.

He feared that a bolt from Zeus's hand would electrocute the cattle stables at any minute, complicating his night further. If the cows got out, or if there was another fire like the one that had killed ten cattle on the Jefferson ranch, he and his wife would be alone in fighting the flames. There was no fire department this far out in the country, and their nearest neighbor lived three miles away. The backcountry in Missouri at night was a dark and unforgiving territory, and twenty miles from the nearest town could pause the bravest men when Mother Nature grew hostile.

Mac's wife, Carol, stood beside him at the window as they looked out with furrowed brows. A flash of electricity over the top of a hill to their north caught a tree, igniting the branches and slowly tearing the giant oak in half. The children, Bobby and Serena, played video games in the next room, quarreling with each other as if nothing were the matter beyond their virtual world. Mac could hear them arguing over who was responsible for the last dungeon failure.

"It's the sixth storm like this in a month, Mac, and I think they're getting worse each time," Carol said.

"I know. Let's keep our heads and hope the storm will pass in a few hours. The satellite shows it's only supposed to be a brief downpour." Mac looked at his phone and saw a dark green mass moving over the spot on an electronic map where their ranch appeared as a little red dot.

He had yet to explain to Carol that earlier in the day, a science reporter for a local television news program had been talking about changing weather patterns soon. Government scientists had been forecasting weather on a mass scale that had not been seen in over five thousand years. This was based on evidence from ice core samples found in Antarctica and the North Pole.

The reporter explained that they were unsure when or how the weather would change this time, but theories that had been circulating for years by what were considered to be fringe outliers and conspiracy theorists were now catching the attention of local newscasters and particularly the attention of a balding man named Ted Trotter, in a tweed suit, who covered the story on an afternoon news program in the Midwest. However, the news station WYAG estimated the total number of viewers to be around three hundred. So, what turned out to be one of the biggest stories in the history of news programming went unseen by almost everyone in America. Still, Mac had been watching and was worried— his time working on Unacknowledged Special Access Projects for the government had taught him more about what may have been coming than he cared to think about.

"It's after ten, and I should get the kids to bed," Carol said.

"Mmmhmm," said Mac.

Carol knew he was somewhere else, and just like when he was at his old job, she could tell there were things he was keeping from her. She shook her head, kissed him, and left him staring into the darkness. Mac watched for a bit longer as his mind drifted back to the laboratory projects he had been working on before he retired from the Air Force. What he could never tell his wife, not only from a contractual standpoint but from a moral one, was anything about the horror show he'd worked on when he and his team were in the catacombs beneath New Mexico. There were too many ghosts and too much carnage along the way. All of that death and violence, just to find what the Consortium wanted: a new Earth. Mac stared into the void, allowing his mind to travel back to those dark times until he felt Carol's hand on his shoulder.

"Are you OK?" she asked. Startled from his trance, he tensed under her soft hand.

"Yeah, I'm fine. I'm just worried about the cattle out there in the barn. This is a bad one."

"They'll be fine, and lord knows we can't control everything. Let's turn in and deal with this in the morning," Carol said.

Mac turned to his pretty wife, gazing into her tired eyes. She was smiling back at him with the hopeful strength that good women in love seem to possess naturally, but the deep black and blue pockets under her eyes revealed just how worn down she was by her disease. Carol's fierce love for Mac was his pillar when he felt weak. He could not imagine life without her by his side. Some loves are eternal, like a flame that refuses to die even against the strongest storm, and he burned for her. Carol knew he had experienced hardships in his line of work in the underground lab. And she knew it must have weighed on him. She sensed, sometimes, that he was broken from his experiences and in search of peace he would never find.

"You're right. We must turn in, and the cattle will be fine until morning. My head is tired, and I need to rest." Mac said. Carol put her arms around him.

"You alright?" Mac asked.

"It's a good day, yes," Carol answered, resting her head on his shoulder.

The cancer that had been eating her away was, they hoped, in remission. Carol lived by her good days and bad since the diagnosis two years ago. Mac and Carol walked toward the bedroom together, pausing to look in on their sleeping children as the storm raged outside. Mac looked at his son and thought of him becoming a man in this terrifying world, which saddened his heart.

"Let's get to bed," Carol said. She patted his chest, and Mac nodded.

Mac lay still, staring at the ceiling, and thought about the thunder outside.

"Have you thought about us getting away from it all for a few days? Maybe travel out to the east coast and hit Myrtle Beach for a week?" Carol asked.

"That sounds like a good idea to me, but what would we do with the cattle while we're gone?" Mac asked.

"We could hire Don Syminski from the next farm to help. He came out a few weeks ago to introduce himself and told me that he and some other ranchers help when people go on vacation or get sick and can't care for their farms." Carol said. "I guess that would be alright. We need a break." Mac replied. He finished her back rub, and they kissed goodnight.

Mac rolled onto his side, closed his eyes, and again, fell into the same nightmare. He was running down a hallway in the underground lab as a dark and unspeakable horror gave chase. The unseen fear was gaining, and as he turned around, his breath stopped; his feet became frozen in solid cement, and he fell to the floor on legs of rubber. Mac began to see multicolored streamers reaching out from within a black hole, like fingers from the outstretched hands of doom. They reached for him, wrapping around his arms and legs, pulling him in as he screamed. His sleeping body turned over, and with the left knee, he kicked Carol in the small of her back. She woke for a moment, tapping him on the shoulder.

"Turn over! Stop kicking me." She said in a half-awake mumble.

Mac was far beyond the reach of her voice as the darkness overcame him in the hallway outside the research lab. He was transported through a portal to a grey planet orbiting a dim star. He lay looking at a cloud-filled grey sky, and as he stood up on the colorless rocky plain, he knew home was a million miles away. Somehow, he had crossed into another dimension when the impossible darkness had taken him. Mac was now garbed in a red robe with gold bands around the cuffs and bottom. Runic symbols were stitched into the cloth in ornate patterns with purple and yellow thread.

A puddle of water had pooled in a crater by his feet, and as he gazed into it, he realized that his face had transformed into that of a white wolf, but his hands remained human. The hood gathered around his shoulders, and he could see purple sparks dancing in his eyes as his reflection glared back at him.

Mac looked up after a time and realized that he was not alone. He stared into the eyes of a large Minotaur, standing not ten feet from him. The well-muscled bull man looked at him with kind eyes, and Mac knew he looked familiar. The silent exchange between their locked eyes was a telepathic signal, and Mac could see them running across battlefields, stepping over the dead and dying and fighting shoulder to shoulder against an army of undead abominations. They had tasted the cold victory of many battles together, and Mac remembered his name was Yxx, chief of the Minotaur clan.

"We are well met, you and I, Mac!" Yxx said. "Where am I?" Mac asked.

"The question is, where will you be, my friend?" Yxx chuckled. His smile was inviting, and Mac knew this was a man he could share many beers with as they sang about the victories and sorrows of war.

Mac began to walk toward the bull-man, but as Yxx reached out to take his hand, Mac was pulled back into the darkness once more. Now, he drifted alone in deep space, curled in the fetal position. Stars and planets whirled around him in their eternal celestial precession as he froze into a solid block of ice and drifted. Silvery, metallic ships suddenly appeared around him, blinking into being with eerie inhabitants, watching him in the blackness as he floated alone.

Mac snapped upright in bed; convinced spiders were crawling all over the floor, sweating, breathing in labored gasps, and terrified to put his feet down. He wiped a river of sweat from his brow and looked toward the bedroom window, only to see the sun had not yet risen. Carol was sleeping beside him, her eyes fluttering a little as she dreamed her night away in a peaceful state of REM. Mac calmed his racing mind with relief, and when he leaned over to kiss her on the cheek, he saw their alarm clock read five-thirty. He would need to check on the cows and get to work before sunrise.

He stood up, put on his pants, and dressed quietly so as not to awaken Carol. Then, he walked out into the kitchen to start some coffee. Mac started the percolator and waited as the aroma of freshly ground beans wafted into his nostrils. The sun was beginning to peek over the horizon as he put a couple of pieces of bread in the toaster. He would eat a quick breakfast and then walk the property. Mac had a four-wheeler, but between the dreams he had been having and stress from the condition his wife was in, he felt like he needed a refreshing walk around the acreage.

Before he let the cattle out to graze, he had to ensure that there were no holes in the fence line. Two weeks before today, one of the new titan storms plaguing the country rolled through, sending a massive oak crashing into the fence. It had taken half the day to fix the torn wires, and that was after they got the cows back inside that had wandered through. He shook his head thinking about it and rubbed the beard forming on his unshaven face.

He had gotten lazy about shaving, a ritual he had adhered to every day of his military career, but out west, he was in a different world with different priorities. For the first time, Mac had found somewhere he could be at some level of peace. There were no secret experiments to involve himself with, no human genetic tampering, and best of all, no chain of command or board of trustees to answer to—just his little family. Mac had chosen a hard retirement, even though he was warned cattle ranching was hard work, especially for a man over forty who had never even raised a calf before, but he was freer now than at any time in his life.

While Mac waited for the toaster to pop, he walked into the hallway bathroom to take care of his morning business and looked at himself in the mirror as he did. He felt older than his forty-three years, like an overused washrag faded and torn from a life spent hanging on racks and tossed around in washing machines. His face had a thin, worn outlook. His crew cut hid the graying hair around his temples, and as he gave a mock smile in the mirror, he caught a glimpse of the younger man he used to be. The crow's feet around his blue eyes gave him away.

He sighed, walked into the kitchen, ate the toast without much interest, and then he filled a travel mug with hot coffee and headed out into another beautiful country morning.

Mac walked outside and took a deep breath of fresh air. He sipped his black gold and made a mental assessment of the tree limbs strewn about the property. He walked the fence and thought about the idea of getting away to the beach. It had been so long since the two of them had been away together, and even during his military days, he worked so often that he rarely saw her until late at night or on the weekends.

"You've let time slip away, my friend, and now she's sick. Good going." He said to himself. Mac kicked a stick toward the fence, and when he did, he saw the hole.

Three hundred yards from the house, something had been blown into the barbed wire, removing a large section of fence, which he counted as nine posts.

"What hit you?" Then he heard the mewling in a tangled mess of wire. A baby calf had escaped the stable and was tangled in the fencing.

"What? How did you get out of the stable?

Troublemaker." Mac said.

He could see blood on the calf's body where the barbed wire had torn into her, and as she struggled, the barbs dug in further, increasing her pain and cries. Mac ran inside the house to wake his son and was surprised to see Bobby dressed in his boots.

"Where were you going?" Mac asked him.

"Good morning to you, too. I was coming to find you because I thought you might be out there walking the fence." Bobby smiled and yawned.

"Sorry, good morning; I was just surprised to see you up, was all," Mac said and smiled. "I do need your help. The fence was busted last night, and a calf is tangled up in a mess. I have to cut away the wire before she gets hurt anymore. I wanted you to help me pull it away to get her back to the stable."

"Sure, let's go. You need help putting new fencing up?" Bobby asked.

"Yeah, you interested in helping?" Mac asked. "Dad, we live in the middle of nowhere, and I have three video games. I'm bored if we don't have any work to do around here, and school's not in.

Besides, Serena bugs me all day to play with her if I'm not working, so I'm free to help."

Mac proudly clapped his twelve-year-old son on the shoulder, looking at this miniature version of himself. There was no other feeling like it on earth; he sometimes felt like Bobby was his spitting image: bad habits and all.

"OK, I need to go to the stable to get the wire cutters, and then we can repair that fence before lunch. Have you got something to eat yet?" Mac asked. I had some toast a few minutes ago. I'm good until noon," Bobby answered.

"Hey, Dad, I was listening to a radio program out of LA called Your News AM that was talking about this weather we're experiencing. It's on an internet station, and the guy says this is the end time; it is freaky. He said we've seen so many floods and hurricanes because the earth is about to shift poles or something. He also said that when that happens, the world will flip upside down, and the North Pole will become the South Pole, but before that, there will be all kinds of crazy earthquakes and volcanoes erupting worldwide. Is that true, Dad?"

"This is what you spend time listening to on the Internet?" Bobby shrugged. "Those are just conspiracy theories from guys who don't understand what they're talking about," Mac said with a raised brow.

"Well, he seemed to be fired up about it, saying the government knew about this issue fifty years ago, and they did nothing to prevent it, that sort of thing," Bobby said.

"The weather is a serious problem, but he's probably talking about man's intervention, the industrial age, and the coming climate change. There is no conclusive proof that what we have done on this planet had any effect whatever on the environment or current weather conditions." Mac said.

He told his son this to prevent him from worrying, but his time in the catacombs of the underground lab told him that time was growing short for humanity on earth. It was a difficult situation for Mac, to be a father on one hand, and the former commander of a dark science project,

one that left him permanently scarred, on the other. His mind traveled back to his last subject.

Her name was Mary. That word flashed in his mind like a beacon, and had the soldiers done their job, the drugs should have knocked her out, and she would never have had the opportunity to tell him her name, but she wasn't, and so she did when she was pleading for her life. He saw the serum enter her arm a second after he realized she was conscious.

"Please, mister, I ain't done nothin'," Mary said. "These guys just picked me off the bench I was sleeping on, but I'll find another place to crash."

"I'm so sorry," Mac said.

Mac stood beside her with a white medical mask on, his face frozen with fear as he watched the first side effect of the serum grip her. Mary's head slammed back against the chair; then she began to strain against the wrist straps. The monitor by her head began to show a field of stars and planets as her body convulsed. Her conscious mind was deep in the field of space, showing Mac the solar system, pushing beyond the planets of the Milky Way into a dark void. The final image her mind displayed was two distant stars shining in the blackness, and then, Mary convulsed with so much force that she broke her own neck on the chair's back. The two soldiers who injected her with saline instead of morphine were summarily removed from their positions and placed on permanent duty watching a radar station in a remote part of North Dakota.

He had been assigned to USAP programs involving some of the creepiest experimentation since Nazi Germany, and most taxpayers would probably shoot their congressman if they knew their tax dollars were funding murder. Even if Carol and the kids knew the scary truth of it all, they couldn't do anything about it. The clock was ticking on humanity, and he would enjoy the time they had left with his family in the backcountry.

"So, you think he's crazy?" Bobby asked. "Maybe. I think he has some valid concerns;

we all do, but I wouldn't base my knowledge of world climate on a guy you heard on the Internet without credentials behind his name. You have to be extremely careful where you get your information from and what you choose to believe." Mac said.

"OK, thanks, Dad," Bobby said.

"Last thing I'll say about it. You're going to hear many things from different people, and many of them are based on their agenda."

"Agenda? I don't know what you mean." Bobby said.

"A good example of an agenda is the documentaries you find online, right? I know you like to watch them, and these are people who have a passionate opinion about a topic. They've created a movie to sway you in one direction or another to gain publicity or followers for their movement. Sometimes, these people have a legitimate gripe, and those are the issues you want to research to see how you can help. Still, others are political, and you have to watch out for them because, in the background, corporations are funding these ideas. They may profit when you support the movement without giving back to the people. It's called propaganda, and we've gotten exceptionally good at it as a species. My advice is to research on your own and read books about climate change that have been peer-reviewed by other scientists."

"How do you know so much about all of this?" Bobby asked.

"I've done my time on earth and fallen for enough lines of bull. That is why we live on a three-hundred-acre ranch in Missouri and not in suburbia with the rest of the schmos." Mac ruffled his son's hair and grinned at his rapidly growing little boy. Bobby smiled back with admiration.

He hoped his son would never know how bad it had all become and that he would be an old man before the hammer fell, but there were no guarantees. When they reached the stable, Mac rummaged through his toolbox to find the wire cutters, and then the two of them hiked over to where the little calf was still lying helpless, looking at them with large black eyes that screamed: "*Help me.*" Mac walked into the tangle and stood over the baby animal, gently clipping the barbed wire, and Bobby carefully moved it away from the calf. In thirty minutes, she was free and could stand on her own. The two led her down to the stable, and by that time, Carol and Serena were awake and stood on the front porch.

"How bad is it?" Carol asked.

"I don't know the extent of the damage yet; I only walked three hundred yards up the fence before I found one of the calves tangled in a mess of wires," Mac said.

"Is she going to be alright?" Carol asked.

"I think so. She got banged up a bit in that barbed wire, but it's not too bad. If she starts to look sick, I'll call the vet. We'll repair the fence before lunch; you want to come help us out, Serena?" Mac asked. Bobby shook his head fervently, which made Mac smile.

"Nah, I'm gonna' ride my pony, Wild Fire, after breakfast," Serena said. Mac had gotten her a painted pony for Christmas, and Carol taught her how to ride the small horse. Serena loved the pony and was learning to care for another creature, which delighted her parents.

"OK, no problem. Have fun, sweetie!" Mac said,

"It looks like you dodged a bullet; she got interested in something else," Mac said, laughing. There will come a time when you want her around, and you two will have to rely on each other, especially out here in the wilderness."

"Well, right now, she annoys the heck out of me," Bobby said.

Mac chuckled and shook his head as he walked the calf to her stall, got out his medicine kit, and cleaned the barbed wire wounds. After he finished, he and Bobby put their wire in the back of the truck and motored up the hill to repair their fence. They secured the section in a few hours, and since the sun was getting high in the sky, he and Bobby drove the rest of the property instead of walking. There were no more breaches in the fence, so the two stopped at the hill where the oak had been split by lightning the night before.

"This is amazing!" Bobby said. "I was just climbing this tree the other day, and here it is split in two." He touched the broken tree, feeling the burned charcoal bark under his fingers.

"Nature is an awesome force, and something like this is a perfect example of her power. That was a single flash of lightning." Mac said.

On the hill, they could see almost the entire property and their nearest neighbor's ranch house several miles away. It was a tiny dot of a homestead and barely recognizable from this far out. They stood and peered into the distance. Dark grey clouds were rolling across the landscape, and Mac could see thick sheets of rain to the east coming down into a dense column.

"Hopefully, that will stay right where it is." He spoke. Thunder boomed in the distance where the rain fell. Mac kept his fingers crossed as they sat on the hood of his truck and watched Serena mount up on Wild Fire and trot away from the house.

"I'll give her this. She's getting really good at riding that horse." Bobby said.

"Yeah, Serena's a real natural. You have any interest in learning?" Mac asked.

"Maybe, but those animals freak me out. What happens if it goes nuts and takes off while I'm sitting on top or drops me in a river?" Bobby asked.

"Well, they're brilliant animals, and if you treat them respectfully, you shouldn't have any problems. I can teach you to ride." Mac said.

"I'll think about it," Bobby said.

Mac nodded and turned back to Serena, who was almost within shouting distance now. The ten- year-old girl was giggling with glee as she approached. Mac watched his daughter and imagined her becoming a woman someday with a bittersweet sense of time passing. Her blonde locks waving in her face, brown eyes, and golden smile were sure to charm the pants off any guy; Mac just hoped it would be the right one and not before she graduated from college. Serena was a humorous, intelligent little girl who loved life, seeing the good in others even at a young age. Bobby was a handsome boy with rugged masculinity forming as his maturity grew, and Mac could almost see the man inside the boy struggling to break free. Bobby was headstrong and enjoyed seeking out dangerous situations almost daily. The kid reminded Mac of himself with nearly everything he did. Had it not been for the military straightening him out, Mac would have been another drain on society instead of a father raising two children a lifetime in the military.

"Daddy, I'm getting good!" Serena yelled, as her pony trotted up the small hill.

"You're doing great, sweetie! Keep it up." Mac said.

"Yeah, you look good, Serena," Bobby said, smiling.

"Let's go down and get something to eat," Mac said. He looked at the clouds east of them and got in the truck. Serena raced them down the hill, careful not to ride too close to the pickup truck.

"You know, we could have just picked the two of you up and put you in the truck bed." Bobby teased.

"That's not funny, Bobby. Wild Fire's going to be a big girl soon, and I think you upset her." "So sorry, madam!" Bobby said. He rolled his eyes.

When they got home, lunch was on the table, and Carol looked tired, a little too worn down for twelve-fifteen in the afternoon.

"When's the next appointment with your doctor, sweetie?" Mac asked.

"Two days from now," Carol whispered and sat down at the table with half a sandwich and her hot tea.

"Mommy, are you going to be alright?" Serena asked with wide eyes.

"Yes sweetie, I'm going to be fine." Carol looked at her daughter and smiled, but from the expression in Serena's eyes, Carol could tell she had a lousy poker face. Serena's eyes teared up, and she looked at the floor.

Carol looked at Mac with pain, and he tried to reassure her with his thin smile.

"We'll get you the help you need. There are options we didn't have twenty years ago; advances in cancer therapy have come far." Mac said.

After lunch, Mac put the cattle out to graze, and the four of them watched an ancient comedy from the nineteen-nineties titled *Galaxy Quest* and spent the rest of the afternoon together as a family watching movies. If there were any way to save his wife, he would find it.

CHAPTER 2

MAC HAD ANOTHER DREAM THAT night. He was in the underground catacombs once more, walking down a white hallway in his uniform and a white lab coat. Mac was alone, but he felt the eyes of an unseen audience upon him. Ahead, lying on the floor, was a bloody hand, the thumb and forefinger pointing into a lab room, his old lab. Out of nowhere, a haggard woman appeared in a tattered blue smock.

Her cheekbones jutted through sallow, thin skin, her sunken eyes glared at him, and a gaunt appearance. Her hair hung in greasy strings down the fabric of her gown. She knelt, picked up the hand, and pointed the fingers at Mac, scowling, and then she turned and walked into the lab, dragging her feet, and dropping the hand. It smacked the floor with a sickening Mac followed her, and when he rounded the corner, he saw himself in the same chair he used to have his research subjects strapped into. On the other, he was staring into space, drool rolling down his chin and pooling on his brown T-shirt.

The woman stood with her head bowed, turned away from him. Mac walked closer, his heart racing, dread sweeping through him. He stopped a few inches from her and touched her shoulder. She spun on him with supernatural speed, and he recognized her immediately as his wife. Carol fixed him with an angry glare.

"You!" Carol screamed. "I'm sorry!" Mac Cried. "You let me die!"

He sat bolt upright in bed, sweating, breathing labored, terrified, and crying. Carol lay next to him, lightly snoring as he lay back down. It would be two more hours before he drifted off to dreamless sleep.

The next day, Mac was out front chopping wood when his son walked outside to join him. The air was fresh and sweet on this beautiful spring day without a cloud in the sky. As he worked, a starling sang her sweet melody in the shade tree outside their house. This was a day where anything was possible, and Mac could feel the positive energy as he swung his ax into one hunk of wood after another.

"Hi, Dad, you want to drive out to the back forty today and work on the tree house?" Bobby asked.

"That sounds like a great idea. Maybe we can get to it if I can finish some of this work. Do you want to lend a hand? I also need to go down to the farm supply store and get more dewormer for the dairy cows," Mac said.

"I'll help out," Bobby said and grabbed an ax. "You two come in for breakfast. I'm heading to town later this morning for a job interview." Carol said.

"Interview? Where?" Mac asked, pausing mid- swing.

"The library is looking for some help, and although it's quite a drive, I need something to do besides sit around here and feed you three. It's only a part-time job anyway." Carol said.

"Well, that's OK. Have fun but be careful and good luck. Please call me if you need anything." Mac said before dropping his ax.

"I'm sick, not helpless," Carol said.

The tumor in her brain had been causing violent mood swings, but the doctor had warned Mac that it could happen. Her green eyes flashed at Mac as he held up his hands in defense against her wrath.

"OK, I meant no offense," Mac said. Carol went back inside. "Sheesh, touchy."

"You shouldn't mess with mom," Bobby said. "She's been more irritable lately."

"It's my job to care for her with or without her permission. You'll see if you're lucky enough to find a woman as special as your mother, and I pray you do." Mac said.

They went inside, and the sweet aroma of fresh bacon and eggs awakened their nostrils.

"Awesome, Mom! You cooked breakfast!" Serena cheered as she entered the kitchen from her bedroom.

"Yeah, thanks, mom!" Bobby said. His mouth watered at the sight of the morning feast.

Mac walked over and kissed her on the mouth. This morning, her cheeks were more colorful than the previous day. He came closer and hugged her tightly. This hug lasted a long time, and when he let her go, tears were in both of their eyes.

"Thanks, babe," Carol said.

Mac sat across the table from his wife, his best friend, and as he watched her, his mind slipped back to when they had been much younger and free. Twenty years had passed like a flash in the pan, and here they were, growing old together. His graying hair, her tired eyes, but it had not always been that way. In his memory, they were both twenty-three, and he was driving her to Las Vegas for the first time. They were excited, and the two of them had just been paid. Mac smiled at Carol from the driver's seat, and she looked at him, but he was driving too fast.

One hundred miles an hour through the Mojave Desert, and if he had wrecked another car might not have found them for hours. Mac had the top down on his convertible, and the hot desert wind whipped through their hair as if speeding through an oven. With a single move, Carol unlatched her seat belt and stood up in her seat, holding on to the windshield for life. She scared him half to death, but his smile never faltered.

Carol shouted into the afternoon sun, and they were alive more than ever. That was the summer he was promoted to First Lieutenant in the United States Air Force and took the job in the underground lab. Only months later would his world flip on its ear.

"What are you smiling about?" Carol asked. "That trip to Vegas when you almost gave me a heart attack." He spoke.

"Oh my god! I can't believe you still remember that. We were so crazy back then." Carol said.

"Yeah, well, I think we need to leave for the beach next weekend and get out of here for a few days," Mac said.

"Hey, Dad, someone's coming down the road!" Bobby said.

Mac looked out the window to see a black sedan driving to their house. When it was parked by their front porch, he saw a government plate with the United States seal emblazoned on the mirror finish.

"Great, I haven't finished my eggs, and the ants are at the picnic. This can't be good." Mac put down his fork and looked out the door.

The sedan's rear door opened, and a man in Air Force dress blues stepped out into the midday sun. Mac could tell who he was from his posture.

"Great. It's General Martin." Mac said.

"What do you think he wants?" Carol asked. "You're retired."

"Well, I'm sure it's not because he wants to reminisce about old times. They weren't that great." Mac said.

Bobby was already headed for the front door to greet the ornately decorated senior officer standing in their dirty front yard. Mac sighed and rose from his chair.

"Let's see what the good General wants, shall we?" Mac said to Carol. He rolled his eyes and walked through the door.

"Good morning, Colonel MacDonald! Long time no see." General Martin said.

He was a tall man with an athletic build and graying brown hair. He wore a Cheshire Cat grin almost all the time, and it had always irked Mac. It reminded him of pool hall hustlers and smoke- filled poker rooms. His driver was a butter bar lieutenant who sat behind the wheel trying to listen to their conversation as close as possible in the most inconspicuous way.

"You're a long way from home, General." Mac smiled. He shook the General's hand, admiring the three silver stars on his shoulder epaulets. "Looks like you jumped a few stars since the last time I saw you."

"Good morning to you as well, Colonel MacDonald." General Martin said.

"You're not out here to see my cows, so what's up?" Mac asked.

"We need to talk." General Martin said. Mac led him out to the big split tree.

"That thing took a wallop." The General said. "The lightning storms are getting worse," Mac said.

"These are unfortunate times, Colonel. There are some things about the environment our beloved news channels are not revealing, and for a good reason." The General said.

"Earth's in trouble?" Mac asked.

"Science geeks are saying five years, but I'd put it at more like half that. On top of the erratic lightning, an earthquake destroyed Three Mile Island this morning, and tsunamis are becoming more the norm than an anomaly."

"What do you want from me?" Mac asked. "I'm getting to that." The General removes a black coaster-sized object from his pocket. "This is a corbamite platter constructed for deep space exploration as a holographic communication device. This one was set up as a projector, but we can talk back and forth with them. It's pretty neat stuff. Corbamite is the heaviest element in the world and can't be broken; it's formed in the vacuum of space at zero gravity. Its durability is also perfect for communications when scientists are floating around in deep space far from home, although we have not tested it further than our own solar system yet. We also use it on the skin of stealth aircraft, the international space station, and submarines."

"We were working on some of that stuff before I left the cave, along with the human trials experiment," Mac said.

"Well, the work you were involved with was a huge success, and after you left, we made some tremendous breakthroughs that your team helped push. As I said, you should have stuck around. There could have been a ton of money in it for you." The general pressed a small black button on the device in his hand. A white LED light blinked on the inside, and a 3D model of outer space appeared in the space between them.

"I don't need to tell you that if you mention this to anyone, bad things will happen to your family, right?"

"I think you just did," Mac replied.

General Martin nodded as they both turned to the movie emitting from his palm. In a contained 3D holographic image roughly sixteen inches in diameter, a movie began to play for the audience of two. The stars and planets of their solar system whirled by as the two watched with wide, expectant eyes. The General stared with his caught-the-canary Cheshire Cat grin as Mac cocked his head in amazement. After a few moments, blackness appeared in the depths of the field, and they were looking at a binary star system with a host of colorful planets orbiting these luminescent plasma giants. The camera swung around both stars in a wide loop, displaying the miraculous discovery with brilliant clarity. Mac stood with his mouth open, and his heart began to beat faster as he felt sweat in the palms of his hands.

"You found life?" Mac asked.

"Yeah, and possibly our new home. This is the most recent data we have from the Zeta Reticuli quadrant. What you're about to see is something that few people have." General Martin said.

"OK, hit me."

The vision of planets orbiting in the fabric of space faded to an open field of tall green grass and three travelers walking shoulder to shoulder. Only, they weren't human. They were wolf men who looked like creatures from a medieval fairy tale. They appeared very tall, and he could see their maws extended like the wolf in Red Riding Hood. Two of them carried battle axes, each with a sword slung across their backs. The third one was garbed in a red hooded robe with golden threaded cuffs and purple runic symbols emblazoned on the sleeves. Their progress was halted when the robed figure stopped and looked at the sky.

The robed wolfman turned his eyes toward the camera of consciousness following them, sensing that an omnipresent voyeur was watching. He began speaking to the others in his party, but Mac could not hear them. That was all they could see before the movie darkened, and the LED on the little black projection device in General Martin's hand flicked off. They were left standing in the same field they had been to a few minutes before, but now Mac had seen something he'd never unsee. There was real life somewhere out in the cosmos beyond Earth. His life had been changed forever, and his breath had been stolen. Fear for his family's safety now that he had been exposed to this fascination welled up, and he began to wish the General had never darkened his doorstep. He wondered if there were snipers ready to erase him and his family and imagined them lined up along his roof.

"Was this information gathered from the human trials experiments?" Mac asked.

"Yes, about a year after you left the program." "I don't know what to say. I mean, what are they? And if I don't want to do whatever it is you want, are you going to kill my family and me?"

"The truth is, we don't know yet, but I'll be frank. We need you to go out there, ensure the coast is clear, and then get a cosmic portal back to Earth so we can cross." General Martin said.

"You think they have an oxygen-rich atmosphere?" Mac asked.

"We've had some science geeks in the cave looking at this video for months, and they think it might be. We don't have a craft that has gone out there to get readings for us and determine if the planet is habitable for our people." General Martin said.

"What's a cosmic portal?" Mac asked.

"A little something we picked up from an EBE craft that crashed a few years back. It's a suitcase- sized device that opens the fabric of space-time, and you're mission commander on this one."

"I can't go," Mac said.

"You'll try to find these hairy sons o' guns and make friends. What do you mean you can't go?"

"Mac, we have a ship that can manipulate the crossing point of light and cut the time it takes to get from here to there from over forty years to nine months. You find the planet, feel it out, and ensure it's safe for us to come across. You know, befriend the locals, negotiate a treaty, and then activate the cosmic portal to open the doorway back to Earth. When you open the gate, your wife and kids will be the first people you'll see."

"General, my wife is very sick with cancer, and I just can't leave right now. She needs me, and if something were to happen to her while I was gone, I'd never forgive myself, and there are the kids to think about." Mac said. He was rubbing his chin.

"Mac, we have a finite amount of time left on Earth."

"My wife might be dead by the time I return," Mac said.

"I understand your concerns, but you should take this mission. It's for the greater good, and your country needs you. And also, the last mission commander was killed during testing." "What? Killed, how?" Mac asked.

"We were conducting deep space exercises in one of the light benders, as we call them, and a faulty oxygen line erupted out of nowhere, killing everyone on board. It was a damned mess, and DSEC almost shut down our program." The General said as he bowed his head.

"How far out were they?" Mac asked.

"They were almost to the rings of Saturn when we lost communication with them. The craft has a zero-point return onboard so, if anything goes wrong, it returns to the cave. When we got it back, all of them had depressurized, and the mess was enough to make you lose your lunch for a month." "My God, and you want to do this again?" Mac said. He was disgusted.

"That mission, the ship that failed, was an experimental re-engineered version of the craft we captured from ET. The one you'll be going in is the real deal, Mac, and this one will work. You have my word." General Martin said.

"The answer is still no; I'm sorry, General," Mac said.

"Mac, I understand. I'm not without a heart, and when my wife, Sheila, was sick a few years ago, I was torn up inside. She died too young because the environment we live in is deteriorating at a rapid pace, and our bodies can't adapt to the toxins in it. We do not have another twenty years here, my friend, and it will get much worse before this gets any better. Our only hope is that planet you just saw those wolf men on, and we need to get there. Humans need to be there."

"I understand, but I can't leave my wife now.

Find someone else," Mac said.

"There is no one else. Tell you what, think about it and reply, but don't wait too long. We need to evacuate, soon." General Martin held the hexagonal black plate out, and Mac took it.

He placed it in his pocket and would hide the magnificent device in the floor safe of their bedroom as soon as the General left. Mac felt uncomfortable having it in his possession because he did not want to become a conspirator. The two men walked back to General Martin's car.

"General Martin, Dick, it was a pleasure to see you again," Mac said. He put out his hand, and the General took it.

"Don't wait too long to get back to me." General Martin said.

Carol came down to hug him, and he could see the exhaustion in her eyes. He had never seen her so frail.

"Carol, as always, it was a pleasure to see you." "Dick, I was sorry to hear about Sheila. Dianne Honeycutt told me a little while back." Carol said.

Mac looked at her with surprise.

"You were out of the country, and I was in a spell with the chemo. I forgot to tell you. I'm sorry," Carol said to Mac.

"Thanks, Carol. You two take care." General Martin said and hugged her. He got into the back seat of his car, and in minutes, the black sedan disappeared down the dirt road.

"He wanted you back at work, didn't he?" Carol asked.

"I told him to get bent," Mac said. "Besides, I want to go to the beach with my family." He hugged her, and she fell into him.

"Thank God, I don't know if I can go through that again," Carol said as her right cheek pressed into his chest.

"I have to take off to the Farm and Feed store this morning. Can you call Don Syminski and see if he'll tend to the cows while we're away, please? We'll fly out on Monday, a week from now, and be back by the next Sunday morning. I'll check for flights to Myrtle Beach when I get back from the store today." Mac said.

"Do you want Bobby to go with you? I'll take Serena to the interview with me," Carol said.

"Dad, you're not going without me, are you?" Bobby popped through the screen door and jumped down the three steps from the porch.

"Hah hah! I guess not. Get in, and let's get this done, buddy." Mac said.

Mac got into their pickup truck and turned on the engine as Bobby jumped in and buckled his seatbelt.

"So, what did the man in the uniform want?" Bobby asked.

"Oh, he just stopped by to find out how we're doing and to see if I'd go back to work for him, but I'd rather spend my time with you guys."

"You used to work on some crazy stuff, huh?" Bobby asked.

Mac stayed silent for a minute, reflecting on the years of classified projects, paperwork, and a thousand faceless people.

"I know, I know, you can't talk about it," Bobby said.

"There's not much to tell. I worked on a bunch of boring research projects for the military. I want to focus on getting the feed and dewormer for our cattle and then get away from here for a week. It's time for a long overdue vacation."

"We're really doing it? Going to Myrtle Beach?" Bobby asked.

"Yeah, your mom needs this more than anyone. She grew up near Myrtle Beach, and I wanted to give her a good week away from it all."

"And you don't want to go to Cancun or someplace exotic?" Bobby asked.

"Heh, yeah. I did, but she mentioned that beach in particular." Mac said.

"Dad, is mom going to die?" Bobby asked. He was looking at the floor.

"The doctors are doing everything they can for her," Mac said.

"I'm sorry, Dad. I hear you guys whispering about it, and I don't want anything bad to happen to Mom."

"I know you don't. Me neither. Let's just dwell on the brighter side of your mom's situation, you know? The cancer doctor is going to find a cure for this or help your mother go into remission.

They've got top men working on this, I promise. Top men." Mac said.

"OK, Dad. I think the beach will help everyone relax." Bobby smiled, and Mac hoped they could both get her illness out of their minds.

They drove into town, passing by rundown buildings and slums that used to be a flourishing community on the verge of becoming a bustling city.

"I don't like coming through here much anymore. It's depressing and dangerous after dark," Mac said. He looked at Bobby and then back to the road.

He looked around at people aimlessly milling about crumbling street corners as his truck navigated a minefield of potholes too far gone for simple patch jobs; this road would have to be torn up and redone. Two old men in tattered leather dusters sat under the awning of a convenience store, their chairs kicked back against the wall and cowboy hats covering their eyes.

"Siesta time," Mac said, watching the men. "Don't these people have jobs?" Bobby asked. "The world economy is on the verge of collapse, son."

"How did this happen?" Bobby asked. "Honestly, it's because a handful of evil men have traded us all in for money that only exists as a material object with no power other than what we give it. Years ago, when I was younger, I didn't think we'd have to worry about money. I purchased our land outside of town while I was still in the military, paid everything off and traded half of my retirement money in on in Costa Rican currency. I figured that even if the United States collapsed, I would have a backup plan, but I never anticipated the scale of this. It's all over the world now, not just here." Mac said. His truck slammed into a large pothole and almost sent them careening into a fireplug. "Damned roads!" He yelled.

"So, what goes on down here at night?" Bobby asked. He wanted to redirect the conversation. His father's occasional speeches about a global cabal frightened Bobby more than he wanted to let on.

"There's drugs, prostitution, and a bunch of not-so-great other things that you're too young to know about. Just don't come down here at night with your friends. You know, when you're old enough."

Three old pickups sat outside the Farm and Feed store when they arrived, the rust clinging to them like hungry parasites, devouring the metal beneath. Mac recognized one of the trucks. It belonged to Dale Florence, a dairy farmer whose family lived six miles from him. Dale was a good man who had helped them out when they first move to Farmington. The first winter had been rough and had it not been for Dale and his knowledge of the harsh Missouri winters; their cattle would have died. Mac got out of their truck, and Bobby followed. They passed by a group of teenagers smoking cigarettes outside the store and Mac guided his son by the shoulder into the Farm and Feed.

"C'mon son. Let's go."

The little overhead doorbell jingled as they walked into the farm supply store. An odor of industrial fertilizer mixed with old wood hung in the air. As beams of sunlight shone through the windows, Mac could see dust particles floating through the air like microscopic satellites in orbit—rows of farm supplies lined lightly stocked shelves, another symptom of the community's decline. Dale turned toward them and waved. When the two entered, he had been talking to Fred Selks, the store manager.

Dale had a formidable beard growing, and deep lines formed on his face from years of hard work on the farm. Mac thought he looked like the actor Lloyd Bridges in his later years. Fred was a much younger man in his twenties, and Mac heard that he had taken that job as a manager when his dreams of heading out to Hollywood and becoming an actor had dried up, along with his confidence.

"Hi, Dale!" Mac said.

"Good to see you, boys. You hear the latest news yet?"

"No, what?" Mac asked.

Above the counter, a TV mounted on the wall displayed the evening news. A Channel 8 helicopter circled a smoky patch of land surrounded by water. Piles of rubble dotted the small island where the smoke had not yet covered. "Three Mile Island in Pennsylvania just melted down. There was a nasty earthquake out there, and it sheered the reactors. The whole state is under a federal emergency." Dale said.

"Oh my God! That's terrible; when did this happen?" Mac asked.

"A few hours ago, during rush hour. The President is coming on in a few minutes to discuss what to do next. People are dying out there, a lot of them."

"Guys, here's the news, dude, now," Fred said. The other two men stopped talking and listened. The man on screen was looking into the camera. He had a smart-looking blue tie on under his tan sports jacket. He looked grave, and his tone was serious.

"Early this morning, a 7.5 magnitude earthquake ripped through the Three Mile Island nuclear power plant, and all three reactors have gone into a catastrophic meltdown. Reactor two was shut down in nineteen seventy-nine. Still, it and the other two active reactors have begun to release more radiation into the environment than the Chernobyl and Fukushima disasters combined." A map of Pennsylvania with a big red dot on the Three Mile Island power plant was displayed behind him.

"Reports are coming in that a state of disaster has been declared in Pennsylvania. Lancaster County, Harrisburg, and all surrounding counties have been ordered to evacuate as soon as possible, and residents are encouraged to seek safe harbor in Virginia and Ohio. The Federal Nuclear Disaster Management team is already preparing for the worst, and they have reportedly been sent to the site of the meltdown. President Jim Holley will be addressing the nation in a few minutes from his home in Texas. The president is currently on vacation with his family at their home in Austin. Please stand by and when we know more, you'll know more."

"This is officially the most scared I've ever been, and we're halfway across the country," Fred said. He was running his hands back through his hair, the length of which reached his shoulders.

The men and Bobby stood still, waiting for the next update. When the president finally addressed the nation, he did not have much more to say than general thoughts of concern and sadness for the families affected by the crises. When the brief speech ended, Mac bought his fertilizer, told Dale and Fred good day, and walked out of the store in a daze. It seemed like the whole world was about to be torn apart. He thought about the General's offer as he looked down at Bobby. His little boy was growing up in a world on the verge of a very dark ending, and it saddened him that his children had to grow up in an era like this. On the drive home Mac was quiet and deep in thought as his son sat across from him staring out the window.

"That thing that happened in Pennsylvania sounds pretty bad, Dad. Are those people going to be, OK?" Bobby asked.

"I don't know, buddy. I hope so." He spoke. But he didn't know whether to believe in his reassurance.

Mac's phone rang as they turned onto the highway to return home. It was Carol's call, and Mac answered it.

"*Dad! You have to get home quick!*" It was Serena, and she was crying.

"Slow down! What happened, sweetie?" Mac's heart went into his throat.

"*Mom fell, and she won't wake up! I'm scared, Dad!*" Serena's voice was frantic, and he could imagine the state of terror she must have been in, standing over her unresponsive mother.

"Stay calm; we'll be home in a few minutes," Mac said.

He laid his foot on the pedal and raced toward the farmhouse.

CHAPTER 3

MAC SLID HIS VEHICLE SIDEWAYS into the porch and was out of his truck before the engine kicked off. He ran around the back and up the three steps to their house and saw the front door was open but forgot about the screen and crashed through it, stumbling into their living room. On the way home, he dialed 911 and was told an ambulance would be on the way. Serena was kneeling next to her mother, crying, and holding her hand.

"Mommy fell!" Serena said.

Carol had fallen on her back and hit her head on the floor as she succumbed to the veil of unconsciousness and went into a backward plunge. She hit so hard that the impact split her skull. A small pool of blood formed around her hair like a crimson halo. Mac ran over and winced as his knees hit the floor.

"Carol! Carol! Oh, please, God, no!" Mac could see she was in bad shape, and he could hear sirens in the distance.

"Daddy, she just fell down, and I tried to wake her up. Mommy wouldn't wake up." Serena said. Mac grabbed Serena and held her close.

"I know you did, sweetie. Bobby, can you take your sister outside, please? The paramedics are going to need room." Mac said. His voice sounded very faint to his ears.

"Yeah, Dad. Serena, come on let's go outside." Bobby reached for her hand, and she ran to him, clinging to his waist.

"You kids go on," Mac said. He quickly turned back to his wife, unwilling to let her go. The ambulance pulled up in front of the house, its lights flashing through the windows and against the living room wall. Heavy boots hit the porch, and he could hear them coming with a stretcher and equipment bags.

"Sir, we need you to step out of the way so we can work. I'm sorry," one of the men said.

Mac could not see his face, and even though they were professional and lightning-quick, he felt helpless as the strangers handled his wife, took her vitals, and assessed Carol's condition.

"She fell," Mac said. That was all he could think of saying.

"Sir, we'll take excellent care of her. Are you riding in the ambulance? I saw some children outside, but we can't take them in the vehicle." "Those are, uh, my kids. No, we don't have anyone else right now. I'll have to, um, follow you. Which hospital are you going to?" Mac said. His mind was in shock.

"Sacred Heart. It's about ten miles south of here. Can you drive, Mr. MacDonald?"

"Yeah, I'll be fine. Please help my wife." Mac said.

The two men put Carol on a stretcher and moved her through the living room and out the door. In a moment, she was in their ambulance, and Mac could see that they were sticking tubes in her arms with bags of liquid hanging from the ceiling. Mac motioned for the kids, and they followed him to the family truck, an old Hummer Mac bought at an auction a few years back. It had initially been the property of Uncle SAM during the last war in Congo, and it still had a .50 caliber mount on the roof, something Mac would not remove. He would argue that it was a war machine from birth, and if he ever needed to mount a .50 caliber machine gun on the roof again, he could do it.

"Get in kids; we're following the ambulance to the hospital where they're taking your mother." Mac followed the flashing lights in front of him, dazed and disoriented. Serena sat stoically in the back seat. Dried tears streaked her dirty, pretty face, and Bobby, a born conversationalist, sat quietly in the front seat, staring out the window. Mac flipped on the radio to a local rock station, and his mind flashed back to when he and Carol met. She was sitting beside the base pool, the child of an officer, and he was a young Second Lieutenant. For days, he'd tried to get up the nerve to walk over and talk to her, but he always thought Carol seemed disinterested and bored when she looked his way. He eventually decided to throw caution to the wind one afternoon in July. That day Carol was by the pool wearing bikini top and cut-off shorts that showed off her slender, tan thighs as she sat curled up on a lounge chair, reading a murder mystery. Mac took a deep breath, approached the lounge chair beside her, and asked her out. She told him she never went out with strangers and made him sit beside her.

"When I first met your mother, I thought I was in a job interview. She would not go out on a date with me until I answered a battery of probing questions. That was something else." Mac said to the kids.

"Looks like you passed her test," Bobby said. "Yeah, ha-ha. I did, and it gave me insight into what life would be like with her. I'm glad I passed her first test, but it wouldn't be the last." Mac said. He couldn't think of anything else to say, so he turned the radio up.

They finished the drive in silence. Mac was too distracted to talk, and the radio kept his mind from the creep of panic. When they arrived at the hospital, Mac parked in the visitors' section as the two paramedics burst through their ambulance doors with Carol, unconscious, lying on the stretcher. They extended the stretcher's accordion-style legs and wheeled her inside through a set of sliding double doors that read ER above them. Mac, Bobby, and Serena all walked inside as he fumbled around in his pocket for the phone. He had to reach his sister Lorraine.

If Carol's condition deteriorated further, he would need her to help with the kids. He hoped she would answer his call, but first, he needed to find out where the paramedics had taken Carol. He walked up to the front desk to see a tired, grey- haired woman sitting behind the counter in a white polo shirt with a caduceus embroidered on the left breast and *Patient Services* written beneath that. On her right breast was a name tag with *Pam* engraved. She was on the phone talking and ignored Mac as she gave directions on how to get to the emergency room to the person on the other line.

"Excuse me, ma'am; the paramedics brought my wife through here. Can you tell me what room she'll be in?" Mac asked. The woman paused momentarily, looking up at Mac with an unconcerned and irritated expression.

"Please, can you help me?" Mac asked. "What's her name, sir?" Pam asked.

"Carol MacDonald," Mac replied. Pam stared at her screen and tapped on the virtual keyboard, beaming out from the monitor onto her desk momentarily.

"She's down in the ER triage. Doctor Skinner is looking at her now. He's the attending." Pam pointed down a long grey hallway, and Mac could see the signs for ER leading the way. The medicinal odor of industrial cleanser made the whole place smell like it had taken a chlorine bath. He wondered how many viruses were lurking behind every corner of this house of the sick and dying.

"Dad, is mom down there?" Bobby asked.

Serena was holding her brother's hand.

"Sir, children can't go down to the ER. There are two gunshot wounds and a stabbing down there. They'll have to stay here." Pam said. She was hanging up her phone.

"Daddy?" Serena said.

"They can sit here with me. Do you have any family coming?" Pam asked.

"Guys, I gotta go call your aunt, Lorraine." Mac was staring at his phone as the kids sat on old plastic hospital chairs behind the counter, next to Pam, in a room full of half-sleeping strangers.

He dialed the number and listened as it rang twice.

"Hello? Mac?" Lorraine asked.

"Hey, yeah, it's me. Carol had to be rushed to the ER."

"What? How is she?" Lorraine asked.

"She passed out while Bobby and I were in town for supplies. Serena called me, and she was pretty shaken up."

"I'll bet. How is Serena doing now?" Lorraine asked.

"She's scared. She's worried about her mother, but I'd expect that. Lorraine, I have to leave the kids up front for a few minutes while I go back and see Carol. There are some gunshot wounds and stabbings back there; it's pretty gnarly stuff, I guess. Bad for the kids to see. Although, with what's going on in the world I wonder how long we can shield them from that stuff." Mac said.

"I'll be there in a few hours, just hang in there and tell the kids their aunt Lorraine is on the way," Lorraine said. Mac hung up with his sister and walked back inside the hospital waiting room. The kids were sitting next to Pam mindlessly thumbing through some magazines. He waved to them with a half-smile and surveyed the room full of strangers. Each is waiting for their own version of news from the condition of loved ones or friends secreted away to curtain-veiled cinderblock rooms. He followed the signs toward the emergency room, and as he did a text appeared on his phone from Lorraine, that read, On my way. A little blue dot appeared on the location of Lorraine's house, a red dot showed the hospital location and connecting those dots was a pink line with a moving black icon of a car. Mac felt some relief knowing that his sister was on the way because since they had moved out into the country, there were times when he felt like the only man on earth, especially when Carol had episodes. And she'd never gotten hurt like this before. He placed his phone in his back pocket and navigated the maze of hallways to his wife.

When Mac found Carol, she was lying in a bay with five other people, but the staff had closed curtains around her, which at least provided the illusion of privacy. Although Carol was still unconscious, a nurse had changed her into a white smock and covered her up to the waist with a blanket to keep her warm. A stern-faced doctor stood over her, reading the screen of a handheld medical chart and shaking his head. He was startled when Mac stepped through the curtain.

"Doctor, I'm Mac MacDonald. Carol's husband, please tell me what's happening with her?" Mac asked. The doctor looked up from her chart and turned to Mac with a grave expression. "Mr. MacDonald, I'm Doctor Skinner." He shook Mac's hand. "I'm sorry to be the one to tell you this, but your wife's cancer has spread to her brain through the liver and lymphatic system." "Well, is there anything you can do? You know, like surgery or something?" Mac felt his heart plunging even as the words left his mouth. The doctor cocked his head and grimaced.

"Mr. MacDonald..." "Call me Mac, please."

"OK, Mac. We ran a scan of your wife's vitals and found that her cancer has spread at an alarming rate. It hit her liver and spread so fast there is very little we can do but make her comfortable."

"Her last doctor, uh, Reginald Boxer, told us there was an advanced therapy we could try just two weeks ago. She's gotten worse that fast?" Mac asked.

"Carol developed a massive tumor in her brain that's growing around her pineal gland, and although we could go in and take it out with new methods of brain surgery, the rest of her body is too far gone."

"There's nothing you can do. I don't understand...with all our technology?" Mac said. "Doctor Boxer was going to attempt an experimental cell reversal therapy that uses cord blood stem cells to eliminate cancer cells and replace them with new cells coded for the affected organs or systems within the body. In some cases, with patients caught early enough, we've seen dramatic improvements in health. Two weeks ago, your wife was not showing signs of a brain tumor or a massive spread through her lymphatic system. I'm sorry, but there's nothing I can do. Her body is so weak that anything we try might make the situation worse and kill her faster." Doctor Skinner said.

Carol woke up and squinted. She was looking at the men as they talked with sleepy eyes.

"Well, nobody lives forever." She whispered. Her voice was cracking from dehydration. Little balls of white spittle clung to the corners of her mouth.

"Hey, sweetie," Mac said. He moved around the bed and took her hand in his. It was ice cold.

"How long do I have?" Carol asked.

"A week, maybe two." Doctor Skinner said. He looked at her with a perfectly blank expression. Doctors were always too good at that, Mac thought.

"Thank you for your honesty, doctor. Can I speak with my husband, please?" Carol asked.

"Yes, ma'am. I'm sorry to have to deliver this news. Please let me know if I can make you more comfortable." Doctor Skinner said. He nodded to them and disappeared around the corner.

"You're not planning on leaving me here, are you? I'm not dying in a hospital. You have to take me home." Carol said.

"Yeah, of course, we're out of here, but I don't know what to do, Carol. All my life, I've always produced the answers. This is the first time I've been unsure where to go next." Mac said. She gripped his hand tighter.

"We will take it one day at a time, and I will spend my remaining life with you and the kids. Where are they?" Carol asked.

"They're out in the waiting room. Lorraine's on her way." Mac said.

"That's good because you'll be a mess when I'm gone. Is she staying with us?" Carol asked.

"I think she's staying, but I don't know for how long."

"Call your sister back and tell her to go to the house. I always liked Lorraine..." Carol nodded off again.

Mac walked out of her room and into a nurse's station, where some ladies were working behind their computer screens.

"I'd like to check my wife out and take her home, please," Mac said.

"OK, let me get the doctor, and he'll be right with you." One of them said. She was a small, frail-looking young woman with black rings under her eyes. He wondered how many late shifts this twenty-something had worked. Doctor Skinner walked around the corner as soon as she said the words.

"Doctor, I want to take my wife home," Mac said.

"I thought you probably might, so I prescribed a strong opiate that'll help her with pain."

"But doesn't that mean she'll be high as a kite?" "That's the best I can do, but yes." Doctor Skinner said.

"Alright, thanks, I guess."

"I'll approve her discharge. Take care of yourself and the kids. This is likely going to get worse before it gets better." Doctor Skinner said.

"That's the second time I've heard that today," Mac said.

"Here's the number for grief counselors I've known for twenty years if you need to talk."

Despite the stress, Mac never minded a direct approach and shook the doctor's hand before they parted ways. Minutes later, Carol was awake again and placed in a wheelchair by a well-built male orderly in blue scrubs. Mac walked beside her, looking sideways at the man pushing his wife. He had long blond locks falling in his eyes and had a habit of blowing them out of his face, to have them fall right back down in front of his eyes once more. As Carol rolled by the front desk, Bobby and Serena hopped up with bright smiles on their faces. Mac looked at them with a smile on his, unsure what to tell them.

"Don't worry, big guy. I'll tell the kids tomorrow morning." Carol grabbed and squeezed his hand. He wanted to cry, but he knew he couldn't.

"Mommy! You're awake!" Serena yelled.

Bobby walked over and kissed Carol on the cheek as she hugged him from her chair. Weak arms surrounded her children as she fought another fainting spell to stay awake for her little ones.

Mac drove them all home and filled the prescription for her drugs. Lorraine arrived later that night, and for the next week, he tried to pretend that the normal world still existed as he watched his best friend slowly wither in their bed. Carol wanted to see the sunlight and be out in the fresh air, so Mac set up the hammock on their porch for her to lie in. Bobby and Serena were unsure how to behave around their mother now that they knew the painful truth about her condition, but they both acted out their roles as if any day Carol would stand up and play with them again like she used to. Lorraine had been helping the kids as Mac spun his wheels and fought, giving up. Lorraine approached Mac out on the front porch as he stared at the night sky, his thoughts heavy.

"Penny for your thoughts?" Lorraine asked. She surprised him, and he was jarred out of his trance.

"What? Oh, hey. I'm just trying to wrap my head around this whole thing. I feel like a five- hundred-pound gorilla is sitting on my chest." "You want to talk?" Lorraine asked.

"I don't have a lot to say. I feel like I've already lost her and she's still alive. I never expected how painful this prolonged agony was going to be." Mac said.

His head went into his hands as he let the tears go for the first time. "Why did this have to happen to her? I'd trade places now. Lorraine, I can't get the horror of my past out of my mind, and I can't lose her now. "

"Big brother, I can't help you with the things you did in the past unless you ever need an ear to bend, but I can help with the kids. I'm sorry for you guys, and I'm here as long as you need me." Lorraine tugged on his shoulder, and Mac allowed her to hold him. She had never seen him break down, and her eyes were teary.

Friday night, a week after Carol was discharged from the hospital, Mac was sleeping by her side when he heard a noise in the house. Something fell in the living room, and his eyes shot open in surprise. He looked to his left and saw that Carol was no longer there. Mac's heart raced as he raced out of bed and ran through the darkened bedroom.

"Carol!" Mac yelled.

She sat in the living room, staring out the large bay window into the star-filled night. The twinkling lights glinted and winked back at him as he walked over, confused.

"Are you alright?" Mac asked.

"It's beautiful tonight." She spoke. Carol stood and glided across the room in her white nightgown.

"How are you out of bed? Are you feeling better?" Mac asked.

"I'm feeling better than I have in quite some time. Do you ever wonder how many stars there are out there? How many planets like the one we live on?"

"I know there are others, just not how many. The General wanted me to go find one of them."

"Billions. Millions of billions of Earth-like planets are out there waiting to be explored, with people just like us living there and evolving." Carol said.

"How do you know that? We should go back to bed."

"You know he's right," Carol said. She turned to Mac and smiled at him with the soft features of the twenty-year-old girl he had fallen in love with so long ago.

"I can't talk about it. They'll come for you if they find out I've said anything." Mac said.

"You have to make sure the kids are safe now. This will be hard, but I must leave and need you to go. Lorraine will be here to help Bobby and Serena." Carol said.

"I'm not sure I can do it. What happens to the kids if I don't make it back?"

"Mac, the earth is going to renew itself very soon, so you have to go and save our children," Carol said.

Mac held her from behind, around the waist, as they watched a star fall to earth from the great beyond.

"Make a wish," Carol said.

She turned toward Mac and kissed him softly on the mouth. It was the deepest, most soulful kiss she had ever given him, and he fell into her arms, tumbling through her embrace and into the void. The world went dark as he popped his eyes open and looked to his left, terrified and knowing what he would find. Carol's spirit had moved on sometime in the night, and although her body no longer contained a soul, she wore the smile of a woman at peace. Mac wept as he touched her still, cold face.

Later that day, when the coroner had come, and Carol's body was removed by Everley Brothers funeral home, Mac decided to change his clothes and found the little black metal device General Martin gave him in the pocket of his jeans when he pulled them out of the drawer. During the emergency, he'd completely forgotten to keep it hidden. Mac sat down in the plush chair in their bedroom and clicked the little button on the bottom. He watched as the holographic movie materialized and the camera began to traverse the stars. What he did not know was that General Martin had the mechanism inside programmed to probe Mac's thoughts and consciousness and to send the data back to an application General Martin had loaded on his phone. The General was, in effect, reading Mac's mind when the device was activated, so while his former progeny was watching a movie about planets in deep space, General Martin was finding out whether the commander was ready for his mission to Zeta Reticuli. From the look of it, there was going to be a funeral in a few days.

"OK, Mac, it's time to pay you a little visit. Sorry for the loss, pal, but it's time to get back to work." General Martin said to himself.

The next few days went by in a blur. The kids were asking questions about what happened to their mother, but Mac struggled to address them and left it to his sister.

Three hours before the funeral, he took a walk up the hill to the burnt tree and sat quietly, facing their house.

"Carol, I don't know if you can hear me, but I just wanted to come out here to be alone with you before the three-ring circus of your funeral begins," Mac said to himself. A robin perched on the part of the tree that still stood as he paused. The bird's song alerted him to its presence, and he looked at it momentarily, wondering.

"I don't know how to go on from here, but I want you to know that I'll do what you asked of me," Mac said.

As he sat atop the hill, Mac thought about the million little things he would never experience with Carol again. He could see the curl of her lips when she smiled at him, the diamonds in her eyes when she caught him teasing her. He remembered the way she held their kids—when they were babies—in her arms like she could never let them go. His mind drifted through the wonderful things they did together in their long marriage, and he wanted to pound the earth with his fists. Mac wanted to tear off his skin and curse the heavens; he wanted to throw hand grenades and watch beautiful things die as his rage boiled over. A bottomless hole had opened in his heart that was sucking him in like a vortex as his mind tricked him to experience the sorrow of his friend, wife, and soul mate leaving him forever. Pain stabbed him in the heart, traveling up his body and stinging his eyes as the tears rolled down his cheeks.

He screamed expletives in a tapestry of emotional torment. "I have to go now. I love you, always. I'll miss you."

His world became colder that day, darkened like a tattered black-and-white photograph. He began walking down to his house to get ready. As he did, the little bird flew away.

Lorraine drove as Mac, dressed in his best black suit, and the children in their Sunday church attire stared out their windows in silence. When they pulled up to the funeral home, Serena began to cry and put her head in her hands. Bobby held the little girl as tears rolled down his red face like silent soldiers.

"Come on, kids, let's get this done," Mac said. "Later, we'll get some ice cream," Lorraine said. The offer seemed absurd even as it left her mouth, but she didn't know how else to comfort them "That sounds good, Aunt Lorraine," Bobby said. His voice cracked and seeing them all in so much pain broke her heart. She was going to miss Carol, too.

When they entered the funeral home, General Martin was standing over Carol's coffin, paying respects, as Mac walked up to him. The General was wearing a black suit instead of his dress blues, something Mac had never seen in the entire time he had worked for the man.

"Good morning, Dick," Mac said. General Martin turned around, and Mac could see a tear in his eye.

"Hi Mac, I'm very sorry for your loss. Carol was a good friend. She'll be missed," the general said. Mac extended his hand, believing the sincerity in his voice.

"Thanks, General. None of this has been easy. The kids are having an especially difficult time as well," Mac said.

The General released Mac's hand and then came in for a full hug. Mac could smell his aftershave as the senior officer brushed his cheek. It reminded him of his father's, and Mac was eleven years old again for a split second when his mother had just passed on. Lorraine walked up with the children next to her and Mac put his arm around Bobby. They all took a seat next to Carol's grieving mother, Grace, and Mac placed an arm around her shoulder. She nodded and smiled at Mac and the kids through tears but remained silent.

"I'm sorry as hell about this, kids. It's not fair, but we'll get through it together." Mac said.

The small family stood next to the coffin as their mother lay in eternal rest before them.

"Mommy looks like she's sleeping," Serena said. Mac and Bobby nodded.

The funeral home had done a superb job with her makeup, and as Mac looked at his wife, he thought she looked ten years younger.

Bobby turned his head as tears welled and walked over to take his seat in the front row.

"Mac, is there anything I can do for you?" Lorraine asked. Her long blond hair draped over her left shoulder, and as Mac looked at her, Lorraine reminded him of how much she looked like their mother. Her kind eyes and easygoing manner made these tough times a little easier, and Lorraine was an excellent shoulder to cry on. Although it had been hard recently, Mac found it was always easy to talk to her because she listened with her heart.

"I think I just need to get through today." He hugged her, gave Carol one last look, and took his seat.

Although the ceremony was grueling for him, Mac stuck it out, and the kids managed to hold back their tears until the coffin lid was closed. Mac assumed his role as pallbearer and helped to carry Carol out to the waiting hearse. Lorraine drove them to the gravesite, and as they got out, Mac noticed that the General was right behind in his black BMW.

General Martin walked with Mac to the hearse's back door and grabbed a side with four other men as they rolled Carol's coffin out. Beautiful words were said in her name, and tears were shed as a good friend, sister, daughter, and mother was laid to rest on a sunny Tuesday mid- morning without a cloud in the sky. General Martin was careful to pick his moment, and as the crowd was dispersing to drive back to Mac's house for the wake, he sidled up to his grieving friend. Grace silently walked toward her waiting car and was gone before ever saying goodbye.

"Mac, I know this may seem like an awkward time to bring this up, but have you thought any more about that offer?" General Martin asked.

"What is it you want me to do?" Mac asked. "I don't know, are you onboard?" The General asked.

"Yeah, what the hell if my kids are taken care of? I don't do this unless my children and sister can join me on that new planet. They're what I have left in this God-forsaken world."

"It's done, you have my word. When you open that cosmic portal, your kids will await you. This is a great thing you're doing, not just for your country but for the world. We need a man like you who has seen your things and knows about the projects in the cave."

"Is that nightmare still ongoing?" Mac asked. "No, we shut it down once we found the planets in Zeta Reticuli. No need to spend more black budget dollars when we have a lead on a viable human life-sustaining planet. I know the experiments shook you up, but if it had not been for the C24 serum and the endless supply of vagrants shuffled through that facility, we may never have discovered our ticket off this dying rock." The General said.

"I suppose, but I still have nightmares about it," Mac said.

"Those people we used may have had their brains turned to mush, but I promise you that was the most useful any of them had ever been in their lives." The General said.

"We turned them into fertilizer for industrial farms," Mac said.

"Sure, we had to get rid of them afterward, and emulsifying them was the most efficient way to dispose of a nasty problem. Honestly, I don't know if they were ever used as fertilizer. Last I heard, the barrels were being dumped in the ocean," the general said. The corners of his mouth turned downward momentarily, and he shrugged.

Mac shook his head in disgust; the General had never been one for the social graces of tactful conversation. He was more like a pit bull who would sell his mother to get the job done.

"Are you going on this little quest?" Mac asked.

"No, not this time. I'm more interested in the crossing once you get the cosmic portal fired up and open the door back to Earth. As they say, I'm staying in the rear with the gear, so I'll leave the heavy lifting to you and your crew."

"You'll get another star for this, won't you?" Mac asked.

"Colonel MacDonald, you may get a star for this."

CHAPTER 4

MAC SPENT THE NEXT FEW days getting his affairs in order and spending time with his children, but he was distracted by Carol's passing and the upcoming mission. He explained to Serena first that he would have to go on a long trip. She nodded understandingly. She seemed very malleable since her mother passed on. The little blond-haired girl, who reminded him so much of Carol, was going to be missed dearly by her father. Although he could not tell her what he was about to do, he called a family meeting to clear the air as much as he could without men in black showing up at the house when he left. Lorraine, Bobby, and Serena were sitting in the living room when he came in with a packed duffle bag.

"Mac, will you remove the veil of mystery and let us know what's going on? Ever since the funeral, you've kept a tight lip and moved around this house like a ghost." Lorraine said.

"Daddy, is everything alright?" Serena asked.

She was wringing her little hands together. "Everything is as good as it can be under the circumstances," Mac said.

"So, what's up, Dad?" Bobby asked.

"I'm going on a trip and may not return for about a year. Before you say anything, I can't tell you what I'm about to do, but I can tell you that General Martin will protect you all in my absence, and when I see you again, it will be a brighter day." Mac said. "You can't tell us where you're going, but you're leaving for a year? This sucks." Bobby said.

He stood up with tears in his eyes and ran out the door. Mac's eyes followed him out of the house, his heart clenching with anxiety. This wasn't going to be easy.

"Mac, are you sure about this?" Lorraine asked. "Your kids are like my kids, but that's a long time to be gone so soon after..."

Serena crawled into Lorraine's lap and buried her crying eyes into her shoulder.

"I have no choice. It may be hard to believe, but Carol requested this as her last wish. I love you guys, and I'll be back, but this is something I have to do. I'll be leaving in the morning." Mac said.

"You'd better go get Bobby," Lorraine said.

Mac nodded and walked outside. He did not expect the children to understand without a reasonable explanation, and even though he'd tried to brace himself for this, it was tearing him apart to leave them behind again. Under any other circumstances, it would have been easier. Carol would have known what to say to them. She would have been strong for his whole family. Bobby was sitting on the tractor outside their barn, staring at the ground, when Mac walked up to him. The afternoon air was cool, and a storm was approaching as dark clouds formed overhead. Mac could see lightning strikes to the north of his property.

"Looks like we're gonna' have another big one," Mac said. He pointed up at the darkening sky.

"Yeah," Bobby said.

"I know this isn't easy, but I'll be back. You know that, right?"

"I don't understand why you have to go now. But I guess I never understood your job. I can't stop you from leaving, but can you tell me if this mission is dangerous?" Bobby asked.

"I can tell you I love you and your sister with all my heart and that's why I have to leave. Take care of Serena, and everything will be much better when I get back." Mac said.

"I will, Dad. We'll miss you," Bobby said. Mac reached out and embraced his little boy.

"Are you sure you're only twelve? I could have sworn you were going on thirty there for a minute." Mac said. He chuckled, and Bobby broke their embrace, clapping his dad on the shoulder.

"I'll watch the fort while you're gone," Bobby said. He smiled at Mac, and for a second everything was back the way it had been months ago.

The next morning at 5 a.m. Mac received an encrypted text message on his phone. When he touched the hyperlink provided in the message, a biometric scanner application automatically opened on his phone.

"*Please raise the camera to eye level, hold it an inch from your right eye, and then press scan on the screen of your cellular device,*" a soft female voice said. Mac raised his phone and stared into the unblinking eye of his camera lens. "*Thank you, Colonel MacDonald. You have been cleared for duty and reinstated to your former rank as Colonel in the United States Air Force. Congratulations and welcome back, sir.*"

A moment later, the text message disappeared from his phone, and the scanner application icon that had been on his home screen vanished. The GPS mapping application opened displaying a little blinking light on his screen. Mac began to get excited, and although the circumstances were far from ideal, he still felt twenty years younger, like a conspirator in a great plan. His pulse quickened at the thought of traveling through space. This was why he began working on the special access projects years ago, and now he'd get the chance to do something special, after all those years of wondering what was out there. The location beacon on his phone's GPS was at the end of a blue line stretching off the screen and as he swiped the screen a few times, following the map, the line diverted to an area in the desert with no main highways or side roads depicted on the map. Mac mounted his cell phone in the window mount, connected the radio application via wireless to his stereo, and put the truck in drive. As he came to the end of his driveway something lightly jabbed him in the hip. When Mac placed his hand in his pocket, he realized the coaster-sized black corbamite disc was the culprit, but he could not remember having put it in his pocket before leaving.

"I thought you were back at the house." He said to himself. Mac turned up the radio and drove south. It was difficult to look behind him now. His mind was flooded with the possibilities of what new life he would see in the vast field of space, and the strange and mysterious adventures waiting to be had just around the corner. The more Mac thought about the mission, the more he knew on a spiritual level that this voyage to the stars was meant for him, and every decision in his life had led him here. After about twenty-four hours the GPS map line ended on his phone, so Mac stopped his vehicle beside a gigantic, rotten saguaro cactus in the middle of nowhere. He was running low on gas, had not slept, and it was hot. He turned off the engine and waited. For five minutes nothing happened, and Mac began to feel the desert heat beating down on him through the windshield. Sweat broke out on his forehead, and he could feel beads of perspiration rising on his forearms.

"What the hell?" Mac said to himself.

He stepped out of his truck and into the afternoon sun of *somewhere* in New Mexico and surveyed the landscape. A tan lizard lay motionless atop a flat rock, sunning itself. For miles around him, there was nothing but small heat-tolerant plants, rocks, and seashells. All was quiet and still until Mac suddenly saw a one-hundred-foot wide, two-story tall metallic disk shot by him like a flash of lightning. It raced away, stopped on a dime, and then flew straight up into the sky.

Mac was so surprised by the sudden appearance of the craft that he almost fell over. It came back a moment later and hovered less than fifty yards from him, silent as a ghost. Mac stood with his eyes wide open, and his hands clenched in tight, sweaty fists as three metallic legs descended from craft to ground with a ramp extended from within. Wary and startled, he steeled himself for whatever was coming next. Mac heard boots hit the ramp and watched a figure in a black flight suit walk toward him. He took a breath and squinted. It was General Richard Martin.

"Welcome to Nowhere, Colonel MacDonald!" The General said. He was grinning with that used car salesman smile once more. "Surprised to see me?"

"A little. You always did know how to make an entrance, though."

The General walked over to Mac and shook his hand. "You want to take a ride?" He asked.

"Is this the ET craft? The one you told me about earlier?" Mac asked. He was walking around the front, staring wide-eyed.

"No, it's an alien replica vehicle, just like the one that failed out in deep space with the other crew.

Damned shame about them." The General cocked his head and made a tsk sound with his mouth.

"I can feel your empathy bubbling over.

Where's the real one?" Mac asked.

"Let's go see. Climb aboard Colonel MacDonald. Oh, and welcome back to duty, you were missed." The General said.

"By whom?" Mac asked.

"By me. Hey, before we get started how are you coping with Carol's passing?" General Martin asked. He fixed Mac with a serious empathetic gaze. "I'm ready to get started, so I can get back and see my kids."

"Yeah." General Martin nodded and looked off toward the desert. "Whole damned earth is going to look like this soon, it's irreversible at this point, and it might take thousands of years for the biosphere to repair itself. Meantime, we'll be very much alive and light years from here. You ready to meet the mission team?"

"As ready as ever, when do I get to meet them?" Mac asked.

"In about twenty minutes, let's go have some fun first. It's been a rocky time for you, and I think you might enjoy what I've got to show." The General extended his arm toward the ramp.

Five minutes later they were soaring inside the ARV high above the ground. The General was flying the craft, diving down through canyons, shooting in between buttes, and grinning like a little kid playing his favorite video game. As the ship performed its amazing stunts, their relative position on the horizon never changed. They both stayed upright even if the craft turned sideways or upside down.

"It's disorienting, staying still while the ship moves. I feel like I should be experiencing G's." Mac said.

"This ship creates its own gravitational field, allowing us to move in any direction with no inertia or awareness by our bodies that anything is happening outside. Your eyes see, and the brain registers movement outside, but your body experiences nothing." The General said. They shot out of a canyon and high into the sky, twisting through the cloudless afternoon as Mac sat perfectly still, admiring the deep blue.

General Martin climbed higher until the darkness of outer space surrounded them.

"Is this thing rated for space travel?" Mac asked. "You tell me. Take the stick; it's your turn to fly," the general said. Mac traded chairs with him and began to pilot the craft as they exited the atmosphere.

"Where to?" Mac asked. The vehicle glided with effortless grace.

"Take her out a little way and back in again. We need to get you acquainted with the crew soon. They're an interesting bunch, you'll see.

Best and brightest, we could find that can keep their mouths shut." General Martin said.

"I'm sure anyone crazy enough to volunteer for this lunacy will work out just fine," Mac replied. He circled the globe while reading an LED instrument panel that displayed a red dot where they exited the planet, and a yellow line followed their path.

The General pressed a small button, and the narrow view widened to the entire canopy, allowing them a 360-degree view of space and the beauty of their home planet below them. Mac was over China when he looked out the window to see a cigar- shaped craft floating out to the starboard side of their vehicle. It was a massive ship; Mac figured it must have been a mile long. It was ivory white and glowed radiantly in the darkness.

"What's that? Is it one of ours?"

"Afraid not; I'm not sure which race operates that one, but we've got around fifty-seven races of ETs checking us out. They've been around since the days before the first pyramids were constructed." The General said.

"Do we have any idea what they want?" Mac asked.

"They all do something different here. Some races have been here trying to protect the planet from us; others study humanity like we're bugs under glass. The travelers see us as an intergalactic zoo. There are a few that mine precious minerals deep underground to take back home to their planets. We can't go that deep underground yet, and a war with them would be futile on our part, so we let them help themselves."

Mac also began to see others out there with them, but these oddities seemed more organic, like jellyfish in the ocean.

"Those ships down there, the jellyfish-looking craft, are living vehicles that frequently cross between our dimension and the one next to ours. The pilots are connected to and command their ship through conscious will. We've only ever caught one of these, and that's because a lightning storm took it down. When the pilot died, the ship began to deteriorate almost immediately. The damned thing stank like a rotting whale in the hot sun if you can imagine."

"Up here the whole time?" Mac asked.

"Afraid so, to most of these people, we're a science experiment, sort of a test to see if we'll figure out our problems before we kill each other off or doom the planet. What puzzles me is why they don't interfere physically until we start playing with nukes. Each time we launch one that can leave our planet, somehow the warheads are disabled, and the rockets are dropped to the earth." The General said. "Why would they care if a few nukes are dropped?" Mac asked.

"Well, they have a vested interest, Mac. Some, but not all, the entities are mining this planet for resources, as I was saying earlier. This planet has so much biodiversity that the interdimensional and galactic communities are counting on its survival, but not ours. So, when we fire a nuke, they stop it. After the United States and our neighbors detonated over 400 above-ground atomic weapons back in the last half of the previous century, the sheriff got a little pissed, you could say."

The jellyfish ship began to signal with red, green, and blue phosphorescence that rippled like lights in a swimming pool.

"Let's take her in. We've been out here long enough, and I need to get back to work," the general said.

"You want the stick back?" Mac asked.

"Nope, this will be you full-time in a day or two anyway. You'll be leading a crew of young engineers and scientists out to Zeta Reticuli," the general said.

"Kids? You've got me babysitting?" Mac asked. "I picked them myself. Look, they're young,

bright, and crazy for volunteering to go on probably one of the most hazardous missions in the history of the DSEC space program. They're prepared to get us there or die trying, and that's all I expect from any of my officers. You'll be fine, don't worry so much." The General said.

"My kids are on the line for this mission, Dick." "I guess you better make it there and get that cosmic portal working."

"Where do you want me to land?"

"The coordinates are in the system, just say The Cave."

"The Cave," Mac said. His eyebrows raised. "*New destination is the cave, as requested by Colonel MacDonald. Estimated arrival is fourteen minutes.*" The ship's computer said.

"That's neat," Mac said.

"This thing can also make coffee." The General said.

"Do I get to fly the real thing?" "Yes, you do, today."

"Does it have the same bells and whistles?" "More, actually. It's the most advanced spacecraft ever made that we know of. There are probably more out there, but the one you guys are taking to Zeta Reticuli will flip your lid." The General said.

The two flew on in silence as the craft returned home on autopilot and in less than fifteen minutes, they were darting straight for a cliff face in the middle of the desert. It looked as if they were going to strike when a door wide and tall enough to accommodate the large ship opened instantly, and they passed through the opening. The hangar was alive with soldiers in black jumpsuits, moving back and forth as the ARV came to a stop, and lowered her landing gear and ramp.

"*Please enjoy the rest of your day, Commander.*" The computer said.

"Thanks," Mac said.

"*You're welcome.*" It replied.

"I love this machine. Mac, I almost wish I were going with you on this one my friend. Almost." General Martin said.

"Yeah, I'm sure you're all broken up about staying back," Mac replied. Martin chuffed a chiding laugh. The two walked over to a larger craft than ARV where four fresh, young, good-looking twenty- somethings were standing around, reviewing charts and graphs of quadrants in outer space.

"Ladies and gentlemen, can I have your attention for a few moments?" General Martin asked. The troupe stopped what they were doing, about-faced, and saluted the General. They held it until he rolled his eyes and reluctantly saluted back.

"At ease, please." General Martin said. "This is Colonel MacDonald. He's your flight commander for the mission to Zeta Reticuli. He was also on the project team that helped discover that life exists on other planets. Until this morning the Colonel was retired." The General said. A few of the team were nodding in acceptance, but Mac saw these fresh faces and wondered if any of them had ever experienced an uncertain future.

"Good afternoon. I'm Colonel Derrick MacDonald, but you can call me Mac when we're not standing around any other high-ranking officers. Have any of you ever had combat experience?"

A tall, dark-haired man stepped forward. "Sir, I'm Lieutenant Jack Sparling, Security Engineer, and I spent four tours in Afghanistan during the poppy field wars. I was infantry with the 9th Marine Regiment out of Camp Lejeune. We were called the Hell Razors, because of all the action we saw and survived, sir." Jack said.

"Hell Razors, huh? I've heard of you guys. There was an officer in your outfit named Major Cataclysm, right?" Mac asked.

"The Major was part of a spec ops unit operating mostly in the jungles of South America, but yes, sir,

he started the outfit. I never met him, sir; that was before my time," Jack said.

Jack had a darker complexion and looked like he might have been of Latino descent. A jagged scar ran down the right side of his face from ear to chin, disrupting an otherwise handsome face.

"Why'd you volunteer for this mission?" Mac asked.

"I want to save as many people from Earth as possible from the inevitable environmental collapse," he said.

"What about you? I guess we'll just go around the circle and then I'll give you my why." Mac said. He was looking at a pretty blond, standing a little over five feet tall. She had a late summer tan and blue-green eyes that drew him in. Mac thought about Carol and quickly redirected his eyes.

"I'm Lieutenant Kim Cross, Colonel. I'm the team science officer. I graduated with a Master of Science in biology and marine biology from the University of North Carolina at Charlotte. After graduation, I was head of an oceanic cleanup project in the Pacific Ocean plastic sea.

My research team implemented an environmental plastic collection system that separated organic life from inorganic plastic debris. Still, when funding ran out, we had no choice but to abandon the project. General Martin called me three days after we returned to shore, and it was pretty much a no-brainer. We're screwed if somebody doesn't do something. Plus, this is the opportunity of a lifetime." Kim said.

"Agreed, if you have been watching the news, you know that they aren't telling us half of the real danger. This planet only has about five good years left before we begin to starve and die. So, what's your story, Lieutenant?" Mac asked. He turned his attention to a tall man with a crew cut who resembled Max Headroom. When he spoke, Mac detected a faint Bostonian accent.

"Well, sir, I'm the team engineering officer Neal Jorgenson. I have advanced degrees in robotics and mechanical engineering from MIT. I've spent several years creating biological robots in an underground laboratory for Synden, a military weapons manufacturer and R&D company. I took the mission because who wouldn't want to rocket out into the cold void of space and risk their lives to save the planet they came from?" Neal said. Mac nodded and gave a silent chuckle.

"Ok, fair enough. I'm sure all will have a good time." Mac said.

"Yes, sir, I can't wait to start," Neal said. He flushed a little, and Mac thought he was a shy man. Neal seemed like the kind of guy adept with numbers and mechanical devices but bad with people.

"Last but not least, I'm guessing?" Mac said.

He turned his attention to a five-foot-three brunette with captivating brown eyes, short hair, but not too short, and a flip to her bangs. Her flawless skin hid her age, and he guessed she could be between twenty-five and forty.

"I'm Stephanie Brandt; I'll be the ship's medical officer. I've treated soldiers on the front line in four wars. If you get sick, injured, or blown up, I can help. I've also got a daughter, and she's the reason why I'm going." Stephanie said. Mac saw that Stephanie was the only one with Captain's bars on her uniform.

"Great to meet you, Captain. Were you commissioned right out of college, or did you bootstrap out of the world of the enlisted?" Mac asked.

"I was commissioned right after graduation. My other friends went on to make large sums of money in plastic surgery or cash-only clinics, but I chose borderline poverty to serve my country and never looked back." Stephanie said.

"That's the harsh truth. Well, it's nice to meet all of you. I'm Mac or Colonel, just like all of you. I want to get as many people off the earth as possible before the end. I've got two children, and I'd like to see them reach adulthood. In my prior career, I worked on a classified project that gave the General the intelligence he needed to put this little search party together. I also understand that the last mission was a catastrophic failure, but I trust this one will succeed. I'm a damned good pilot, my style is to lead, not boss, and we'll get along great as long as everyone is pulling his or her weight." Mac said.

"Great!" General Martin shouted. Let's go to the briefing room and get you up to speed on what you're up against, shall we?" General Martin motioned toward a black glass-covered room.

The small team followed the General across the hangar. When he got to the door, he looked up at what looked like a View Finder toy bolted to the wall. A green laser scanned his eyes, and the door slid back, allowing them access. Mac was first behind the General as they entered a presentation room, where a triangular projector control was sitting in the center of a long white table.

"Colonel MacDonald, each of your team members has prepared a presentation to fill us in on the various aspects of this program. We're calling it Project Phoenix because of the mythical bird that sets herself on fire, dies, and is reborn anew from the ashes of her predecessor. Before we do that, though, let's all take a look at what we are trying to accomplish," the general said. He pointed to a suitcase-sized object in the far-left corner of the room.

"I'll bite; what is it?" Mac asked. "That's the cosmic portal. As you may remember, Colonel, we captured it from an ET spacecraft in 2056, and it took us two years to figure out what it does. This baby opens a cosmic portal or an inter-dimensional doorway. We've been able to attune it to our global positioning satellites and triangulate spots on Earth to test it out." The General said.

He walked over to the device and dragged it to the front of the room. Then he produced a small, thin computer tablet about the size of a credit card from his left front pants pocket and began to tap on the tiny screen.

"Just a second, everyone; I'm putting in coordinates for the last place we opened the gate. You have to be incredibly careful when you use this device. We lost a few good scientists when they miscalculated the longitude for El Segundo and accidentally opened a hole in space. They were sucked through, and we never saw them again. " The General said.

He tapped twice, and the device began to make a whirring sound, like wind through an open grass field.

"That's comforting news. How's it work, General?" Mac asked.

"We have a rough idea. It seems to pull energy in from the field of energy that surrounds us and moves through all life: Time-space, consciousness-related energies. I'm sorry to say that the metal used for this device is superior to anything we have on Earth. We think, but can't be sure, that this device has a memory function. We know there's an organic life form living within. We found it using high-resolution scanners; we can't get inside yet. I believe— and so do some other engineers—that we have a being of higher consciousness contained within this case. We also suspect that this cosmic portal will record the journey from here to Zeta Reticuli and keep track of any asteroids, planets, or space debris you avoid along the way.

We've tested it here on Earth and found it accurate at avoiding freeways and large buildings as the gate opens. We don't want to be wrong about where this cosmic portal opens either because if you open it and the doorway is too close to Saturn, we risk pulling part of that planet in through the gate or collapsing both our planet and Saturn in on each other. We don't want this to go sideways or not as bad as last time anyway. Also, don't lose the remote." The General said.

General Martin held a small remote about the size of an electronic car key and pressed a little button. When he did, two golden rings appeared in the room, one in front of the other, and began to rotate, one clockwise and the other counterclockwise. The space between the rings wavered until a desert scene appeared before them, and suddenly, they were looking out onto a rocky butte-filled scene.

"Where are we, sir?" Jack asked.

"Welcome to Sedona, Arizona. This little device in my hand communicates with the cosmic portal, and whatever the bearer of this remote thinks about is what the doorway opens to."

"That's a neat trick," Kim said.

"It's no trick. Walkthrough, go ahead. You won't get trapped out there unless I press this button again. Oh, and make sure you're on the right side of the cosmic portal before pressing the close button. I almost didn't mention it, but I figured it would be on me if I didn't, and you accidentally stranded yourself in an uncharted star system." General Martin said.

Mac was the first one to enter the desert. The air was hot and arid, and the ground was covered in rocks, sticks, and seashells. What interested Mac was a sun painting on the side of a cliff thirty feet from him.

"That sun was painted over nine hundred years ago. We found out when I opened this door the first time, and a tour group was going through here talking about these cliff dwellings. I heard enough to learn about that sun over there and then shut the gate before any of them saw me." General Martin said. "Well, you all need to leave soon, and we've got some more to talk about. Shall we return to the meeting?"

They stepped back through the doorway, and a moment later, the wall materialized once more. It could have all been a dream except for the scorpion that had followed them back through the portal and was now wandering around in the conference room.

CHAPTER 5

O NCE THE TEAM WAS SEATED again, General Martin asked each crewmate to explain each part of their research to the other members in an effort to educate everyone on what was known up to this point and get ready for the long voyage ahead. Kim Cross was the first one to stand and take the projector controller in her hand. She stood to the side of the screen as the projector's intense light bulb shone a still image of a twin star system.

"This is Zeta Reticuli, a binary star system that has been, thus far, unexplored by manmade craft. However, we were able to secure live images of this fascinating system through the human consciousness experiments that Colonel MacDonald was overseeing under Project Nightingale. Before subject 3092N expired, we were able to go further than we ever have with the project and produced the images in my presentation." Kim said. An image of a twin star system began to grow larger and clearer.

"What the project team was initially looking for were shadow objects that passed in front of the stars that could tell us there was something large orbiting them, like a planet. The trick was to find a planet that was in the Goldilocks range that could support life. Once we zoom in you, begin to see dramatic changes and some interesting features." Kim pressed her presentation clicker button and the star to the left enlarged until they could all see a multitude of planets orbiting a large star.

"What you see here is Zeta 1, and off to the right, big surprise, is Zeta 2, these stars are roughly 39 light years away from earth. You can see them with a telescope, but what the telescopes won't pick up are the four planets orbiting Zeta 1. One of these planets contains humanoid life, and therefore, we suspect it has an atmosphere much like that of the Earth; we just don't know which planet yet, as we were unable to identify it through subject 3092N's visions. The radiation levels between the two stars are low enough to sustain life, and we estimate them to be between six to eight billion years old." Kim said. As she spoke, the General placed a small platter on the table, much like the one Mac had in his pocket. It displayed four planets orbiting Zeta 1 in a perfect hologram.

"As I said, we have no idea which one of these planets supports human life from our view of them externally. Before subject 3092N became non- viable and stopped showing us images from Zeta 1, we saw three *wolf men* dressed in medieval garb walking across a grassy plain. Yes, you heard me right." Kim said.

"Well, I suppose we couldn't expect the entire universe to look like us, right? If we don't come at them with weapons, maybe they won't mind a bunch of strangers landing in their front yard." Mac said.

"Positivity is a good thing, Colonel, and I'm glad you feel that way because you're going to be our public relations officer." General Martin said. "You didn't think you'd just be flying the craft, did you?" He was grinning again.

"Befriend wolf men on a foreign planet when we don't know if they even speak our language?" Mac said more to himself than the others. "Do we know why we couldn't capture their planet during the consciousness trial? Those wolf men may have been a part of 3092N's hallucination as his mind began to break down." He said and looked at the General.

"We do know they're real based on the integrity of the subject's mind at the time of discovery. Why aren't there any telescopes out that way, you may ask? Well, the DSEC lobbied against exploring that space after reading the records of the Sumerian kings unearthed during a war with Iraq in 2010. Allied soldiers found hundreds of clay tablets written in ancient Sumerian containing the stories of extraterrestrial genetic manipulation and cloning of early humans and a bunch of other classified information that I can't talk about." General Martin said. Neal Jorgenson stood and walked to the front of the room.

Neal nervously cleared his throat and scanned the room momentarily before speaking.

"I'm going to, uh, discuss the *Poseidon* and her capabilities, because in my experience as a mechanical engineer I've never seen anything like her before," Neal said. He took the remote from Kim and moved the presentation forward. A large metallic disc appeared on the screen.

"Have any of you flown the ship yet?" Mac asked.

"We've taken her out a few times to test out the *Poseidon's* capabilities, but nothing major. The ARV that killed the last crew was modeled after this one, but I'm sorry to say, we don't have a complete grasp on how this craft functions. What we do know is that it operates on zero-point energy, in other words, it pulls free energy for propulsion out of the quantum field for use in her hyper-drive intergalactic engine."

Suddenly, a major dressed in a flight suit burst into the room.

"General, I apologize for interrupting, but there's something you have to see. A terrorist group just blew up two nuclear reactors in Japan, and seven in the United States. It's mass chaos, sir!" The Major said.

"Alright, briefing postponed. What's this fresh new hell?" General Martin asked.

He pushed a button on the projector, and the image of the *Poseidon* vanished, giving way to a reporter in a grey hooded jacket and red bowtie, a glum expression plastered on his face.

"*A newly emergent terrorist group calling themselves the Chaos Order has shut down energy production centers in Japan and for one quarter of the United States today when they detonated briefcase-sized atomic weapons at three reactors in Fukushima, Japan, and seven here in the United States.*" The reporter said. "*This latest attack comes on the heels of a new bill which collapsed the IRS, World Bank, IMF, all private banks and credit lending institutions into the Federal Reserve Bank, making the Fed the largest financial institution in the world. The Fed was also granted the power of property seizure for default on private home loans, with an addendum that grants authorities the right to imprison citizens in financial default into mass detention camps set up by FEMA years ago.*" He spoke.

Then he showed a helicopter image of a black crater where a small city had once been. The smoking, charred remains of a million hopes and dreams were reduced to a nuclear nightmare. The screen glitched and wavered as the reporter's image was replaced by a dummy in a suit hanging from his neck off from a replica capital building in Washington, DC. An unseen person off camera began to talk in a robotic voice as the dummy began to catch fire and burn.

"*This latest decision made by Capitol Hill has extended the ruthless power of a minority of scoundrels who mean the people of this world great harm. The vile are content hiding in the shadows waiting for their time to strike. While this won't make much sense to most of you, we live in a world already crumbling under the boot heel of a unified elite who have orchestrated and financed every major war for more than five hundred years. These monsters are hell-bent on enslaving the people of this world. Chaos Order has a solution to the problem, and it is fire. You elite few think you'll be safe in your bunkers below ground, secreted away from the rest of the filth you look down upon, but when your children's children emerge from below ground, those of us who survive will be ready, and while new eyes adjust to the sunlight above ground, we will gouge them out and end your mongrel race. This is the end of your game. There are no demands, no amount of money you can pay, and there is nowhere to hide."*

The image of the reporter came back into focus, and it seemed to everyone that the young man had not experienced any disruption on his end because he was still reporting with a nasal, downtrodden voice. More images of ruin appeared on the screen as charred bodies littered unnamed city streets devoid of life.

"Oh my God!" Kim said. They looked at the mass destruction being shown from a helicopter, miles from one of the destroyed sites.

"I am now getting news that we have some video footage of what appears to be a cell leader from Chaos Order. Our policy here at KPPX is to prevent our viewers from witnessing such mass devastation, but currently, we are being held at gunpoint by one of the terrorists." The reporter said. A second later, a loud bang could be heard from somewhere behind the camera, and a dark red hole opened in the reporter's forehead. The images of ruins

and rubble behind the dead reporter changed to a map of the United States where there was a big red dot on Missouri over the Callaway Nuclear Power Plant.

"My kids," Mac said. A white streak of terror ran up his back as he thought of his children being murdered by a psychopathic terror group.

"Colonel, we'll get your children and bring them here. We're forty stories underground in the bunker, and nothing can get through those walls. Major, we need to act fast. Get a chopper and evacuate Colonel MacDonald's family out of Missouri," General Martin said.

The General handed a piece of paper to the Major. Mac could see his nametag read *Stevenson*. He looked back at the screen. The camera was now trained on a man in a snarling wolf mask. He had a black leather jacket zipped up to his chin and was holding a semi-automatic handgun as he stood in the center of the frame.

"Greetings, good people of the world, and welcome to the New World Order, part two. My name is Intolerant Mass." The man said through his mask. He walked back to where the reporter had just been shot and pushed his slouching corpse off the desk.

"We are Chaos Order. It is time that we had a little discussion with you about the stinkfest hell our elected officials and corporations have thrown us into. The little red dots you see behind me are targets of interest, and since nobody listens unless you use a big stick, we decided that this would be the best way to get your attention. Today's events and the previous video were only a small

demonstration of our power. I can assure you now that all nuclear power stations and electrical grids will be offline within the coming weeks and months." Intolerant interlaced his fingers on the desk as he spoke. *"The power brokers of this age have come to their inevitable and timely end. We, the people of the world, the huddled masses of slaves who have had their eyes blinded to the truth for far too long, have had enough of the bull. We prepared a movie to show you where you came from, and while you sit and watch in denial, remember, the wealthy elite, hiding behind their wall of lies, already knew this information a long time ago."*

Behind him on the screen was a movie showing large, ornate spacecraft descending from the heavens and landing among a crowd of apelike men and women. These primitive people were fearful and backed away from the craft, running to their caves and hovels for cover. Landing gently on the stony ground, walkway ramps extended from the ships to earth. Seconds later, giant men and women donning gold-plated battle armor strode down the ramps. They looked upon the cowering masses who remained with disdain as they took several males and females aboard their ship. The next images were more evolved, upright walking men and women, with the facial features of the apelike figures. These people were slaves, working in mines far underground, and what they brought with them from the dark recesses was one cart after another of gold ore. Giants, more than ten feet tall, stood by with whips and hard leather straps to beat the slaves that got out of line.

"What you see here is the best-kept secret of the human race. Extraterrestrial humans came here—to earth—to mine gold, and when they grew tired of doing it themselves, they genetically engineered us to do it for them. It has been going on ever since.

This all began more than thirty thousand years ago, and we feel it's finally time to take power back." His head rocked from side to side behind the Storm Trooper mask as he spoke.

"Let's see what's happening at the Exxon refinery in Waco, Texas, right now," he said.

Images of a large oil refinery appeared, and after a minute or so, little figures could be seen running from the plant. Seconds later, a massive fireball exploded into the afternoon sun, sending pieces of refinery sky-high. Men on fire ran until their legs could carry them no further and they dropped in heaps of burning flesh. Intolerant began to speak once the disturbing images cut away.

"Now, I know what you're going to say. The people in these images had nothing to do with the powermongers who have held us in their financial chains for so long, right? Well, with every revolution comes a few casualties. The governments of this world, run by ancient and powerful families from the royal Anunnaki bloodline, call it collateral damage as their war machines cause untold damage to generations of innocents barely eking out an existence on this planet. Meanwhile, politicians go on glad-handing each other and maintaining the charade that we are all born equal and free. The truth is you have always *been free, and we are about to release you from their chains!"* Intolerant said.

A scuffle could be heard in the studio. Intolerant stood, aimed his weapon, and fired. Then he tossed a hand grenade somewhere behind the camera's eye. It exploded, momentarily knocking out the sound in the studio and rocking the camera.

"Cops are like ants at the picnic. We're taking down the establishment brick by brick; there is nothing anyone can do about it now. Anyway, friends and neighbors, that's all I've got, and if you'd like to know more truth behind the lies, go to this website." A website address appeared below his face, directing people to a truther page, and then the picture faded away, and he was gone. Static hissed on the screen as the feed went dead.

"Ladies and gentlemen, the people of Earth have officially lost their minds. We need to get out of here and get this mission underway." Jack said.

"Roger that, Lieutenant," Mac said, nodding. "You can guarantee my family's safety, General Martin?" Mac asked.

"They'll be here when you open the gate. I promise, and that goes for you, too, Captain Brandt. We know your daughter is in Pittsburg with her grandmother. We'll get her here. Now, the rest of you were chosen because you don't have any family unless there's something I need to know about." General Martin scanned the room, but nobody else had anything to say.

"So, what now? How do we get the ship to Zeta Reticuli?" Mac asked.

"Sir, you'll pilot the ship until we get to approximately 155,000 miles from Earth's moon, and then we'll go into hyper-sleep while the ship opens a gravitational warp and takes us from one end of the universe to the other. The entire trip should last about ninety-one days, but due to the lack of physical space onboard—and our need to eat when awake—it's either hyper-sleep or we starve to death," Kim said.

"Sorry to have to shotgun this information past you, Mac, but this is a project we've been working on for two years. We should have been there and back by now." General Martin said.

"Let's get moving then. It looks like we don't have a minute to spare. World War III is knocking on our front doors, and we've got children to save. See you when we get to our destination, Dick." Mac said. He stepped away, got dressed in a flight suit away from the team grabbed his duffel bag filled with clothes and other gear needed for the long trip. "We had everything ready for you weeks ago, because I hoped you'd make the decision to go. I just wish it weren't under such crappy circumstances. Carol will be missed, Mac. Godspeed, Colonel MacDonald. Be careful out there, and remember your training, if it looks like a duck and quacks like a duck, it's a duck." General Martin said. Something was written in his expression that Mac could not place. Was it fear? Then the General's face became stoic.

"Yes, sir. See you in a few months." Mac brushed off the comment about his wife; it was still too soon, and he was trying to keep himself together for the sake of his new crew.

"We're *all* counting on it." General Martin said.

Mac was in the captain's chair of the captured alien spacecraft in minutes. The ship was stocked with weapons, water, food, and first aid. Jack hid the cosmic portal in a clandestine compartment on the floor, sliding a thin metal plate back over the hole. After he did, there was no evidence that the panel existed; in fact, there were no rivets, bolts, or separations on the entire ship. It looked like it had been poured in a refinery as a single unit, but it had a smooth matte finish metal that Mac had never seen before. There were human-sized pods at the back of the craft, and his eyes traveled down the devices to multiple tubes running to some sort of generator. There were no controls on the dash in front of him, just some flat areas on the console and a few buttons with hieroglyphs on them. A widescreen displayed the hangar outside.

"Those pods are the hyper-sleep chambers where we'll sleep during our journey," Neal said.

He smiled, but Mac wondered if any of them had ever been placed in a coma-like state for any length of time.

There were no hand controls on the flight console anywhere. "How am I supposed to fly this thing with no stick?" Mac asked.

"Here, Colonel...Mac, try this." Stephanie said. She moved her hands over the panel before him, and the ship rose from the floor, suddenly hovering above the ground.

The landing gear retracted as Mac played with the touch controls of this magnificent machine.

One accidental quick swipe drove the ship forward in the blink of an eye, but he stopped just before slamming into a hangar wall and killing three workers who were stacking crates.

"Whoa! That was interesting." Mac said. He gave a sheepish grin as he looked around at the crew standing there watching him. "Let's try that again."

This time, he sat back in his chair and looked outside the clear dome at the hangar and beyond the doors to the open desert.

Mac focused and slowly moved his right hand in a gentle motion over the sensitive touch panel and moved the ship forward. The craft glided like a hockey puck on a frozen lake. When they cleared the hangar doors, he instinctively placed his hand on a panel to the left, and the craft rose high into the afternoon sky. Moving his hands over the left and right panels gave Mac total control over the vehicle, and in a moment, the spaceship darted forward like a bullet from a gun.

The crew sat and watched their new commander quickly master the *Poseidon*. Then, they were off toward the stars, leaving the only home they knew behind in a bid to save their future.

"So, what do we do now? I imagine you all get to sleep through this trip, but what about me? Do I have to fly this thing for three months?" Mac asked. The earth was far below them as they were speeding toward the moon.

"Do you have one of those little plates made out of corbomite?" Stephanie asked.

He reached into his flight suit and felt the little disc.

"Place it on the console, Mac. Watch this; it is so cool." Neal said.

"Yeah, I love it," Kim said.

Mac placed the small black disc on the console and waited.

"Think about Zeta Reticuli. Just free your mind and see the twin stars." Kim said.

Mac let his mind flow, and the twin star system appeared in his mind. As it did the stars appeared to hover above his corbamite plate.

"And that's your autopilot," Stephanie said. "You leave that there and the ship communicates with the energy you transferred to the corbamite plate with your thoughts."

"That's incredible!" Mac said. He was staring slack-jawed at the corbamite disc with his head cocked to the right side as Zeta 1 and Zeta 2 glowed before him in a palm-sized three-dimensional hologram.

"Look, Colonel! Out the right side." Jack said. They were passing the moon, and as they did,

Mac could see ships rising off a location on the moon's surface that he estimated to be the size of a small city. "That looks like a mining colony of some kind. Are those our ships down there?" Mac asked.

"We were told that was classified when we came up here with the General last week, but I doubt they're ours. Look at the size of them!" Kim said. They were all looking now as their ship careened by the odd-looking assortment of massive spacecraft and large land-based vehicles creating mile-wide tracks in the dust and space debris far below.

"See the blue lighted area above the guidance panels; you'll touch that to put us in hyperspace when we reach 155,000 miles from the moon," Neal said. He showed Mac an increasing digital counter and placed it on the console. "The craft will wait until then to send us through the bubble. Also, I don't know how he knows this, but the General told us that you don't want to be awake for this part of it unless you're used to time travel, so it's a perfect time to shut down in our pods." Neal said.

"I'm for that," Mac said. "Alright, you guys hit the hay, and I'll wait to make sure this all goes as planned." The crew began to get into their pods while Mac watched what they did so he could repeat their steps.

As each officer climbed into their pod, the respective doors slid shut over them, sealing in the astronauts. Through the glass, Mac could see that a white gas was delivered inside the respective pods, and in seconds, the crew was in hyper-sleep. The *Poseidon* had a high dome, and Mac could see a three-hundred-sixty-degree view of the stars twinkling far out in the void. As Mac turned to look back the way they had come, Earth was a distant little ball of blue and white, and the moon looked like a child's marble. But something was following them. Mac looked closer. It was the massive ship he had seen lifting off from the moon coming in their direction. With frightening speed, the alien moon ship was gaining on their much smaller craft.

"What are they? Who are they?" Mac said aloud to himself.

An image of tiny onyx-colored men about twelve inches tall flashed into his mind. They stood upright, had two arms and legs, and appeared humanoid, but their heads were bulbous in the back, and they had long, pointy faces. Their eyes were almond-shaped, and he could see the beings communicating verbally as if he were inside the craft with them.

He saw that they had rows of needlelike teeth lining their minuscule mouths. Mac got a sense that they were not friendly and that his ship had come too close to their clandestine mining operation on Earth's moon. The beings aboard the other ship seemed to be communicating with him telepathically, and he suddenly felt their intention to destroy his crew and him. Mac touched the blue lighted panel on his console, and a wavering bubble appeared in the blackness of space before them as he made for his pod. A blue flash of plasma exploded in the space beside their craft as the approaching alien ship fired upon the *Poseidon*. He would have been thrown to the floor without the gravitational field within their craft.

The *Poseidon* seemed to communicate with the holographic image on the corbamite plate and the image of the Zeta Reticuli star system. A translucent sphere, the head of a circular tunnel three times the size of their craft, appeared. Within it, he saw brilliant light for a split second, and then, another blue ball of plasma exploded behind them as the *Poseidon* was drawn into the gravitational pull of a space-time tunnel. As they entered the tunnel, the blue light split into all colors of the rainbow like a prism and streaked past him with frightening speed. What Mac did not see was that as they entered the time slip, the enemy ship gave up the chase and turned back toward the moon. Mac's pod closed over him as their ship was sent along an interstellar highway of pure light that was so brilliant and affecting that he began to experience nausea. Mac's door shut, and as it did, the inside of his hyper-sleep pod filled with the sweet smell of vanilla misting around his head. Mac thought of home, his children, and Carol as he was lulled into a long, deep sleep. Just as his eyes were closing, he could see Carol in the brilliant light and their children, and she was holding them in her arms.

"I'm coming home," Mac mumbled, and he slept. The tiny corbamite plate on the console held the image of Zeta Reticuli, but now inside the hologram was a multi-colored ball of light. Had any crew been awake for the experience, one might have wondered if that ball of light was the exit point for their journey through the cosmos.

CHAPTER 6

IN THE DARKNESS OF HIS hyper-sleep pod, Mac dreamed of a far-off land where he and his children were reunited again. It was a brand-new world, one where the sky was blue, and the air was free of pollution. Mac sat cross-legged in a field next to his smiling son Bobby as Serena played with an odd creature that appeared to be a large mole about three feet tall, standing on hind legs. Both played a game of ring around the rosy together.

Serena was waving a long pink ribbon through the air and laughing as she ran in circles. As he watched his daughter, a large Minotaur, possibly ten feet tall, sat next to Mac and laid a hand on his shoulder, pointing to Serena and chuckling good- naturedly. The Minotaur handed Bobby a small sharp knife crafted with a bone handle. White fluffy clouds rolled across the azure sky as Mac, sitting in the middle of the two, put an arm around his son's shoulders. Mac was wearing brown leather pants, and a white cloth shirt made of old, sturdy linens tied with a thin drawstring around the neck.

On his feet were black boots crafted from dragon-scale leather. To his dreaming mind's eye, the boots' texture reminded him of alligator skin. From around his neck hung a gold chain, and on the chain was the wedding ring he had been wearing when he was married to Carol. On both sides of the ring were small rows of sharp teeth from some predatory animal.

As Mac looked on with a glad heart at his daughter playing in the field, dark clouds began to roll in from the west. His brow furrowed out of sudden worry, and like a page turning in a graphic novel, he was now standing on a field of battle beside the Minotaur wielding a large battleax. Mac was the wolf again, ghost-white and snarling, prepared for war, and at the tips of his fingers were long black claws. The enemy soldiers were fuzzy, nondescript creatures blurs he could not quite make out, like a mirage in the desert. He could see what looked like cavalry, but they seemed to exist somewhere between reality and fantastic imagination.

Mac waited for the first battle cry as wisps of fur stirred in the gentle breeze. Two more figures arrived at Mac's side. They were the warrior wolf men he had seen in General Martin's corbamite captured movie. Snarling and vicious, they were taller than him with knife-like two-inch claws at the tips of their fingers, long muzzles, and sharp, gleaming white fangs.

The wolf on his right looked down at Mac and bared his teeth with approval, then turned his attention back to the inevitable carnage coming their way. Mac was scared, his pulse was rapid, and he tried to stave off tunnel vision as the adversary came into view. Then in an instant, he was gone, far away from the battle. He floated among the stars like a baby in his mother's womb until he was rudely awakened by the opening of his pod and the friendly eyes of Lieutenant Jack Sparling.

"Good morning, sir! We sure are glad to see you awake. The rest of us were awakened by the ship when we hit Zeta, but you were asleep for hours after your pod opened. We were beginning to wonder if you had gone into a coma." Jack said. "What time is it? Where are we?" Mac asked, his voice shaky and cracked. His head was swimming, and he felt like he had just been awakened from a three-day bender.

"We're in the Zeta Reticuli star system. Take a look out the window." Jack said. He was grinning from ear to ear.

Mac stood up, noticing the hunger in his belly first and then the wobbliness of his legs as he attempted to walk toward the window. He rubbed his temples and the months of sleep out of his eyes and looked out the dome at a large blue planet roughly three times the size of Earth. There were huge clouds rolling through the atmosphere, and he could see continents of lush green surrounded by blue oceans.

"Lieutenant Cross, as our science officer, what do you make of this planet? Is this the one we're looking for?" Mac asked. He was groggy and famished and was digging through the crate of MRE's they had brought with them. He settled on beef stew with mashed potatoes and peas, and as a bonus, he got a stick of gum with his meal.

Mac knew they might find other habitable planets on this journey, but it was hard to believe that this could be one. Kim was holding a pistol- sized gun in her hand with a mounted digital readout.

"What's that?" Mac asked.

"This device reads atmospheric conditions and can tell me if the planet supports human life." "Well does it tell you if the air is safe? Can we land on this planet and not die, in other words?" Mac asked.

"The air has higher than acceptable methane gas levels, but that could just be the region I'm scanning. At the very least, we could check it out. Our flight suits will protect us from most atmospheric conditions and the helmets in our bags will filter out harmful gases while they concentrate low levels of oxygen to breathable levels for humans." Kim said.

Mac noticed that the corbamite plate resting on the console now displayed the image of a single star and four planets revolving around it. The largest of them was closest to the crew.

"This device seems to track us by our current location as well as our intended destination. I suppose we'd better go check it out since we're here now." Mac said.

Mac felt his adrenaline rising, and an electric anticipation surged through the crew as they came closer to the large blue planet.

"We may be the first humans on record to have visited this place, it's kind of exciting, right?" Stephanie said.

"It's the adventure of a lifetime. I think that's why we're all here." Mac said.

They were through the planet's ionosphere and descending through a thick bank of white clouds. The *Poseidon* flew with such a smooth motion that to Mac it seemed as if he was on a funky astral escalator.

"This is so cool!" Mac said. He wished he had been given a script to read, like Neil Armstrong when he stepped out onto the not-so-barren landscape of the moon and delivered his immortal quote *one small step for man*, but in the absence of TV cameras and speech writers, *this is so cool* was all he could think to say.

The *Poseidon* glided below the cloud layer. To the west, they could see a canyon, and a few miles beyond lay a massive industrial city. Columns of smoke rose high into the sky, bleeding their gray and black into the pure white clouds. As Mac stopped the craft with a gentle motion of his hands over the controls, they hovered, watching.

"Well, where do we go from here? What's your scanner read Kim?" Mac asked.

She pointed the pistol-shaped scanner at the canyon and city. "It looks like the methane has dropped to acceptable breathing levels in the canyon area and beyond, but out here, they are still a little too high. We might want to get closer," Kim said.

Mac steered the *Poseidon* toward the canyons, and as he did, the crew saw a translucent wall glimmering in the sunlight like a glass shield. Mac tried to steer out of the way, but it was too late, and they collided with the almost invisible shield. It was like moving through a waterfall as the wall spread around them, allowing the *Poseidon* through and then reforming once more as they passed. Kim checked her device.

"Oh, wow, there's no methane in here." Kim looked puzzled. "This dome must have blocked it. Oxygen levels are normal outside right now. This whole city is in some kind of bubble. See how the cloud's part around it?" She shrugged.

"I'm not comfortable landing in that city over there. I know I don't have any experience dealing with extra-terrestrials, but most earthlings would shoot before asking basic questions if an alien craft were to land in their front yard. I can only speculate what the people of this planet would do if an alien craft plopped down and strangers suddenly came out of nowhere, asking for help. I imagine it would not go well. Let's land in that canyon over there and get a better look." Mac said.

"But we're not talking about walking down to the town, right?" Kim asked.

"Yeah, the closer we are to our getaway car the better," Stephanie said.

"We should be prepared to bug out pretty fast if this all goes south," Neal said.

"Everyone calm down, I just want to look through the telescope to check things out a bit so that we *don't* rush in there and get ourselves into trouble," Mac said.

"Well, we have the plasma rifles if things get too hot. Also, we need to make sure we don't get ourselves trapped in between those buildings down there." Jack said.

"You all have a point, and that's why we're going to work as a team to make sure we're as safe as possible down there. That's if we go at all."

The *Poseidon* glided to a flat spot atop a butte, and the crew got out.

"The air's sweet here. The temperature's not too bad, either. It reminds me of spring in North Carolina." Stephanie said. She put a pair of binoculars up to her eyes to get a better view of the city below them. Her digital reading inside the binoculars told her the nearest building was ten miles away. "I do not see any movement. Should we get closer?"

Mac was standing with hands on hips, surveying the area. "It's dead out here, except for these cockroach-looking things that appear to be interested in us." Mac stomped one with his boot and wrinkled his nose as green pus splattered on the ground. Ten more appeared to replace the dead one.

"What the hell are those things?" Jack asked. Twenty more came up over the edge of the butte.

"I'm going to assume they're trouble. We might want to continue this observation from another location." Mac said.

Stephanie walked to the edge of the butte and found millions of tiny bugs covering the cliff face. "We've got a lot of company coming,"

Stephanie said.

Mac was stomping more of them, and now the entire crew followed suit. "Back to the ship!"

They all jogged back as their path of egress was covered by the swarming, green-blooded cockroach bugs.

"You think they're dangerous?" Neal asked. "No idea, Neal, but when odd little bugs display that much curiosity, I automatically assume they don't have my best interests at heart,"

Mac said.

"They look hungry to me," Kim said. More of them clambered over the side. "This is getting scary."

Neal was pulling up the rear as everyone ran up the ramp, and he fell into a pile of encroaching insects.

"Guys! They're all over me! Get em' off! Get em' off!" He screamed and jumped wildly, slapping at his suit and knocking them off by the hundreds. Mac was terrified; he hated bugs. He felt helpless as his engineering officer jumped up and down, screaming.

"Get over here, Jorgenson!" Mac screamed.

"I think one went down inside my suit! Yaaaaaaaaaaggggggghhhhhh!" Neal screamed, panicking. Mac ran out into the swarm to retrieve Neil. He knew it was against all common sense and now feared for his well-being. The cockroaches were on the ramp now, and as Stephanie and Kim brushed them off with their boots, Jack raised the ramp several inches.

"Lieutenant, you need to get your ass on board. Now!" Mac screamed. He tried to still his terror as he stomped across an ocean of little bugs. "Damn, these things came on fast!" He spoke.

Mac slapped Neal's remaining roaches off, looped his arm around Jorgenson, and walked back to the ramp with him.

Once inside, they buddy-checked each other to ensure no more were on them or the ramp and entered the craft. Mac raced to the control console, and their ship was airborne in seconds. Looking through the dome window, they could all see that the tiny cockroach bugs had begun to abandon the butte. Images of a legion of those strange little insects paraded through Mac's mind as an involuntary shiver ran through him.

"I'm not going to sleep for a week after that.

That was crazy!" Kim said.

"Same here, I don't think we met the welcome committee," Mac replied. "After that, I don't know why, but I'm willing to throw caution to the wind. Let's go check out that city and see if this place gets any better."

"You think this is the planet from the video?" Jack asked.

"Somehow I doubt it because I don't see the same environment here that we saw in the corbamite movie. Something seems...off." "Maybe it was the swarm of bugs that just almost ate us," Stephanie asked.

"That didn't help, but it just feels too quiet."

They flew over the city and saw that the streets below were vacant. The only movement was from the smoke exiting a chimney atop a manufacturing plant on the northern end of town. The city was lonely, quiet, and empty.

"There's an odd vibe here, guys. I can't explain it, but I think something bad happened." Stephanie said.

It was an industrial town, and on every street, there were restaurants, apartments, and little shops, all constructed from corrugated sheet metal, rising above yellow brick wall bases. Back on earth, cars resembling those from the nineteen 1950s sat adjacent paved sidewalks, waiting for their owners to return. But there were no people or other creatures outside.

"This looks so Earth-like. I never imagined we'd see this so far from home. You think the people here are humans?" Kim asked. No one answered.

"What kind of readings are you getting on the scanner?" Mac asked.

Kim looked down at her pistol-shaped environmental reader. "Air's fine outside. We could get out and walk around right now."

"Well, how are we fixed for weapons, Lieutenant Sparling?" Mac asked.

"We've got nine nuclear cell-powered plasma repeater rifles with a maximum range of three hundred yards. They're not super long-range weapons, but they'll make their mark. Each one has a night vision scope that can see in zero light darkness, and the rounds fired will put a barn door-sized hole in anything composed of fleshy matter." Jack said.

"So, we won't run out of ammunition?" Mac asked.

"Not for a hundred years if you fired them non- stop every day, all day long," Jack said.

"That's comforting," Mac said, nodding his head. "Let's land around here somewhere and get out near that plant since it's the only place where anything is happening. Maybe the locals are holed up there, or all work in that plant during the daytime."

"Or maybe those cockroach things got them," Neal said. He had a sour expression, and Mac looked back with a furrowed brow. Although it was a morbid thought before they got out there again, he had to consider it an option.

Mac landed their ship in an alley wide enough to accommodate it, and as the ramp descended, Jack handed each of them a plasma repeater rifle. As Mac stepped out into the late afternoon light, he noticed an acrid, rotting smell in the air, like meat thrown in the trash and left forgotten for a week. Tall grey buildings formed the city behind them, and a gentle breeze blew through the lifeless streets. Mac looked to his left and saw a small diner with a blinking neon sign written in a language like the hieroglyphics on megalithic temple walls back on Earth. The entrance to the plant was fifty feet in front of the crew, so they all walked shoulder to shoulder in silence. Mac thought they all looked more like old west gunslingers than a crew of scientific explorers.

"Does that reader of yours also pick up viruses and bacteria?" Mac asked.

"It does, but it will only register known bacteria and viruses, so although it has more than five million potential threats in the onboard database, it won't catch something we've never seen before," Kim said.

"OK, that's not at all comforting considering we are on a planet never before seen by at least modern-day humans, but good to know. Everyone use your best judgment in there and stick close; we have no idea what we're up against."

They approached the big industrial door while Mac led the pack. Jack Sparling covered the right side of the door, and Stephanie Brandt the left side. The door was constructed from steel and had a hexagonal handle that turned when Mac grabbed it. He pulled the door, and it swung open on well- oiled hinges, revealing a long, spacious hallway with fluorescent lights illuminating their path but no signs of life. Mac looked back at his crew to reassure himself that they were still there and stepped inside.

The five of them walked at a slow, deliberate pace, their rifles at the ready position, until they came to a large auditorium. Inside the darkened room, chairs filled with people faced a lighted stage. Mac could see their heads and elongated craniums coming to a point at the tip of the skull, and the odor of stale rot filled the air with toxic fumes.

"They're all dead. This is a tomb, not a manufacturing plant, and it must be on automatic power somehow." Mac said. Something moved in the shadows at the front of the room, up near the stage.

"Sir, there's something in there. Let me go first, please." Jack said. Mac nodded and allowed Sparling to move to the point position. After all, Jack had been a combat soldier, and it made sense to allow him to go first.

"Hello? Is there anybody in here?" He had his rifle ready. "We're here to help," Jack said. He knew that was a lie, but if someone were in need, they might come out if they thought the cavalry had arrived.

Jack walked through the room, and when he reached the front, he dropped his weapon and knelt to pick up the perpetrator of the noise. The others worriedly squinted in the darkness.

"Nothing to worry about from this guy," Jack said. He picked it up and showed them the frightened creature. "Looks like they have cats here."

"You don't know that's a cat, Jack," Kim said. "It could be a shapeshifter or something more awful."

"Yeah, right. This thing is terrifying." Jack rolled his eyes, placed the cat on the floor, and as it ran off, it meowed back at them.

"What killed these people? I don't feel right about this place, and I don't think this is the correct planet. We should go." Kim said. Neal started coughing like something was caught in his windpipe and bent over, placing his hands on his knees.

"Guys, I don't feel so well," Neal said. He lurched forward and vomited dark, dense, slimy matter onto the floor. It splattered with a sickly slap like tar being ejected from a machine. Then he fell to his knees, rolling over on his back. Blue veins were running up his neck toward the temples.

"Neal!" Stephanie shouted.

"Stay back from him; we have no idea what he's got!" Mac yelled. "Neal, your neck!"

As Neal lay on the floor, one of the roaches popped its head out from under the collar of his space suit, and another crawled out of his open mouth. Neal made a choking, gurgling sound and struggled to get off the floor as two more of them appeared next to the one perched on his lower lip. He batted them away in horror and tried to stand up while spitting two roaches onto the ground.

"They're inside him!" Jack said wretching, as they helplessly looked into Neal's terrified eyes.

"We have to help him," Mac said. He was stunned, however, and had never seen anything like the horror before him.

Neal tried to get off the floor one more time as his mouth worked to get words out, but then with one final breath, he collapsed and died nine light years from home in an alien manufacturing plant. The roach things escaped Neal's mouth and skittered into the darkness, secreting themselves away from the vengeful feet of the space explorers.

The small team stood silently, looking down at Neal's body, mourning their sudden loss. Jack got an idea and walked into the auditorium flashing his light on the faces of the dead. The people of this planet looked almost human were it not for their elongated heads and almond-shaped eyes. Death and desiccation had stretched the skin so tight against their skulls that their silhouettes were stiff and rigid, like figures in a wax museum. When the light hit one of the aliens in the face, a curious roach popped its head out of an eye socket.

"I know what killed the people in here. We need to run!" Jack yelled. He ran for the door as the rest of the team chased him.

"We'll have to leave Neal. I'm sorry." Mac said. He was in a fast jog and on their heels were a few hundred cockroaches. Their numbers were growing as the team ran for the ship.

"Let's just get out of here before any more of us end up like Neal," Kim said, breathing heavily as she hustled along with the others.

They burst through the door, and as they did, the ramp descended. They could see that the buildings were covered in cockroaches, and the path to their ship was disappearing rapidly.

"When we get onboard, everyone strips! We're not taking a chance that any of those things get off this planet," Mac screamed. He was last onboard with Kim in front of him. She jumped for the elevating ramp, and Mac followed a second later. The craft rose from the ground and hovered twenty feet from the street.

"Everyone, shuck your suits, now! We have to make sure none of those roach things are inside our suits. We're all adults here, so I expect you to act like it. Underwear, everything, off, now. We're going to do buddy checks. Ladies, you can check each other and hop into the latrine. We'll stay out here, but this happens before we leave. Those things killed Neal pretty quick, and we cannot risk another incident."

The crew found no more bugs inside their suits, and after everyone regrouped and calmed down, there was time for an emotional release and a small ceremony for Neal. Mac said a few words about him as they performed a mock burial and went around the circle, each telling their own story of how they best knew Neal. Mac then consulted the miniature corbamite plate and their holographic image of the star system for the next closest planet for investigation. They had not yet ascended to outer space as the *Poseidon* cruised over the cockroach planet, still beneath the protective oxygen bubble a mile from the ground, when they passed over some crumbling monuments. There was an ancient obelisk and what appeared to be pyramids in the dense jungle below.

"There are pyramids down there!" Jack said. "He's right; they look very familiar, too," Kim said.

Mac motioned for the binoculars by making a *gimme* signal with his upturned fingers, and Kim handed them over.

"There are six of them that I can see, and three look like the pyramids in Egypt with some possible Indonesian influence. But you could put the other three in Central America and not tell the difference between these and what the Aztecs built. This looks almost exactly like one of the lost human cities," Mac said.

Long forgotten by the inhabitants and in disrepair, the pyramids had become victims of entropy. The jungle was encroaching, and thick vines wrapping around their ornate, decorative architecture would soon hide these magnificent edifices, burying them from even the sharpest eyes in the sky.

"Should we go down to check it out?" Kim asked.

"Time is short, and I think we've checked this planet off our list. Besides, I'm not endangering any more lives by exploring ruins with those carnivorous bugs running around. It's a shame. I don't know how anyone could survive here with this infestation running rampant. These people made it for years up until recently. These ruins look old as hell." Mac said.

"I wonder how they got here, the bugs, or what caused their creation?" Jack asked. "Maybe they were victims of their technology, just like us. The bugs could have been a byproduct." Stephanie replied. Each crew member nodded in agreement.

"Or maybe the little critters came in on an asteroid, life from beyond. Many people think that's how the flu and other viruses we find difficult to kill arrived on our planet." Stephanie said.

"Whatever caused it, this place is a bust. We'll leave it to some other poor unfortunate souls to find." Mac said.

With one last look at the pyramidal structures below, the *Poseidon* was off in a flash and whipping through space again. *Poseidon* shot toward the next planet as the crew followed an elliptical pattern around Zeta 1. The dark was eerie, and after losing Neal all aboard were more homesick than ever. Mac felt the darkness creep into his heart and tried to send some good thoughts and energy toward his family at home. The only light came from the brilliance of Zeta 1, and as they seemed to drift into the stillness of the void, her light was beautiful and radiant, but foreign and unknown. From the captain's chair, Mac felt like he was inside a ride at an amusement park just waiting for the big hill to come up around the next turn. The next planet came into view, and as it did Kim began to point her environmental scanner at it.

"Anything?" Mac asked.

"No, we're still too far out, I guess." She spoke. It was a big brown ball in the distance, and as they got closer, Mac thought the color did not change or get less blechy. At least that's what Serena would say when she was three and looking at something that did not sit right with her. "That's blechy, daddy!" The memory made him chuckle and took him away from the strangeness of their new reality for a moment. The distance from Earth was further than any of them had anticipated, not just in physical distance but in emotional proximity to loved ones. He feared that space madness could ensue for him and his crew if they did not find the new home planet soon.

"Thinking about your kids?" Stephanie asked. "How'd you know?" Mac replied.

"I had a hunch. I've done nothing but think of my little girl since we left Earth. I'm putting my faith in the idea that the device we're bringing with us will open a door back to her. It's terrifying, you know? The idea of failure and the collapse of humanity on Earth. Maybe I'm overthinking it." Stephanie said.

"If you're overthinking, so am I. But we'll carry out the mission and complete our task. I want to see my kids just as much as you do. I would not have come on this quest if I thought we'd fail." Mac said. She nodded and gave a wan smile.

"It is beautiful out here though, isn't it? I mean, we're so far from what we've ever known, but it's exciting to see for the first time what so many never will." Stephanie said.

Mac agreed and looked out the dome window as she stood beside him. Her brown hair almost touched her shoulders, and he wondered for a moment what it would be like to put his hands on them and hold her from behind as they stared into the void while he inhaled the lingering scent of her shampoo. Mac's loneliness for female companionship was causing his imagination to work in mysterious ways, and he banished the thought, instead returning his mind to business. He worried that someone might have seen him and quickly looked around. Jack Sparling was watching him with a smirk on his face as if he had read the senior officer's mind. Mac cleared his throat and blushed. Stephanie walked over to chat with Kim a moment later, leaving Mac to his own devices. He stood staring out at the vast beyond alone for quite some time after their conversation. Fighting loneliness, longing for Carol and fear of the unknown, he tuned in to the soundtrack in his mind, playing Steve Miller Band.

Ridin' high I got tears in my eyes
You know you got to go through hell
Before you get to heaven

"Mac, we're getting closer, but I'm not seeing any oxygen on the big brown planet. The atmosphere appears to be hydrogen-based." Kim said.

"That's number two of four that's going off the list," Jack said.

"Still, I wonder what's down there though. There's got to be *something* on that planet." Mac said. He was staring out the window as their elliptical pattern arced around the planet.

"That brown ball looks dangerous, and don't ask me why it just does. I want to move on to door number three, please." Stephanie said.

"How far away is Zeta 2 in case none of these work out, Kim?" Mac asked.

"In this ship, we could be there in a few days or a week tops," Kim answered.

As they passed by the planet, the team watched brown clouds part as a twister rose above the ionosphere, churning like a massive whirling nightmare across the planet's surface.

"That's a hostile environment," Jack said. "Moving on," Mac said.

The *Poseidon* sped away into the cosmic field toward their next exploration in this part of the star system. Unsatisfied, and disappointed by the lack of opportunity this planet presented, Mac took one final look back before they disappeared into the distance. A second later his eyes widened to the size of saucers as an enormous tentacle swooped up from the surface of the planet, attempting to snag their craft. He reacted with quick reflexes and raced to his controls steering the *Poseidon* out of the way before the unnamed horror dragged them down into the depths of the brown planet.

"Did you see that?" Jack asked, astonished. He looked back and froze in horror as a gigantic red eye glared at them from the surface.

"That's not a planet; it's some sort of creature!" Stephanie yelled. Her mouth was frozen in an O of terror as more tentacles whipped at them from the large brown ball.

"Is it coming at us?" Mac asked. Instinct kicked in, and he dodged left and right to avoid the grappling monster, taking the crew to a safer distance. In a moment, they were entirely out of reach, sighing in relief.

"It appears to be caught in the gravitational pull of the Zeta 1 star. Let's get as far from here as possible." Kim said. The planet-sized monster was now a smaller ball of waving tentacles as they escaped from its unblinking red eye and deadly long appendages.

"How does something like that come into being?" Stephanie asked.

"There are more things in heaven and earth, Horatio, than are dreamt of in your philosophy," Jack said.

"Thank you very much, Hamlet," Kim said. "Man, I don't know what it was or how it could even exist. The universe is a vast, mysterious place, and I have a feeling that the things we've seen already are about to get even stranger. All I know is that from the consciousness experiments we performed under my command; I can tell you that we picked up some very whacky stuff from the participants' experiences." Mac said.

"Like what? Can you talk about any of it, Mac?" Stephanie asked.

"Well, here's one, and it's strange. Some of our subjects saw into the crypts of the ancient dead rulers of Egypt. Essentially, they traveled back in time. We learned that the ancients built the pyramids by using anti-gravity technology, and they had help from ET's, but it's more than that. The people of that time were smarter than we are now, more connected with planetary energies." Mac said.

"Pardon me, sir, but those people were living in mud huts and moving blocks of stone with logs, right?" Jack said and smirked.

"That's the story we know that the ancients were superstitious and uneducated hunter- gatherers who painted weird murals and etched their walls with copper tools and sharpened stones." Mac admonished.

"Hey, that's what we're taught in school," Jack said.

"The truth is they knew the stars better than any of us today, and our scientists are just now beginning to catch up to their understanding of math and science. Have you ever questioned how the hieroglyphics are so perfect on the walls of these shrines and ancient artifacts, and the ludicrous idea that copper chisels and stones were used to create such perfect lines? Or, better yet, how they crafted bowls and vases from metals and stones that even our lasers would have a hard time crafting today? You think they did it all with simple hand tools?" Mac asked.

"You may have a point, but I'm just saying, we're not told this stuff even in college archaeology classes," Stephanie said.

"That's the best thing schools and colleges can do in a divide-and-conquer society, you guys. Why would they ever tell the slaves that there's freedom at their fingertips if they can only learn what the ancients knew? I've seen the blocks of the Great Pyramid levitating through the air and being placed just so. The entire structure is only 3/60th of a degree off from true north, and some of those blocks weigh fifteen tons each, roughly." Mac said.

"I've heard of the massive stone blocks at places like, what was it...Baalbek. The blocks there are so heavy we don't have cranes strong enough to lift them today." Kim said.

"I don't know about all that. I mean, we're flying in a UFO right now, but still." Jack said. He seemed perturbed by the conversation.

"Hey, you wanted to know what we were doing, and after some of the things I've seen, nothing surprises me anymore. Why do you think the General sent me?" Mac asked.

"We figured he needed an old timer to keep us in line, I guess," Jack said. He shrugged and blushed.

"Rude! That was uncalled for." Stephanie said. "No, it's all right. I walked away from the project when I began to see more and more people getting their brains scrambled by the drug cocktails we were injecting into them. To push their consciousness further out into the field, we had to up the game. We had people so far under we were sure we could get them to the God Head if we wanted to, but it was a fool's errand. When my time in service was up, I told General Martin to go to Hell and moved to a cattle ranch with my family."

"So, they found this star system and planets after you left?" Jack asked.

"That's right. I didn't even know about this ship. Compartmentalization: it's how the government gets it done. Well, the people who run the government anyway."

"So, you're a conspiracy theorist, too?" Jack asked. He began to feel like he was treading on thin ice making such an accusation of a superior officer.

"Hah, no, I'm not a conspiracy theorist. Who do you think funded this little trip? Do you still think it was the Air Force or the Marines, or maybe the taxpayers voted to send us out here?" Mac asked.

"The Deep Space Exploration Consortium did, but they're a defense contractor and beholden to the laws of our government, right?" Jack asked. He began to feel like that answer was wrong as well.

"You're right about the first part. The second part is untrue because DSEC is a group of multinational banks and families that control the majority of the world's wealth. The bloodlines go as far back as the Anunnaki and biblical Nephilim. These power brokers are the same ones who wrecked our planet with their misuse of power, and now we're their dogs looking for a new planet to colonize."

"That's crazy. I mean, it sort of makes sense when I think about it, but the fact that they let it go so far, that *we* let it go so far, it's..." Stephanie said.

"So, what happened to the great pyramid builders all over the world? If you ever saw what happened, I mean." Kim asked.

"As far as we could tell, it looked like there was a global war at some point. Misuse of land combined with ancient super-technology..." "They wiped themselves out," Jack said.

"Yeah, and they don't plan on doing it a second time, but if it comes to that again, this time they'll flee the nest and leave the rest of the rats to drown," Mac said.

"Sir, the next planet is in view," Kim said. She had been looking at the corbamite plate which tracked their movements and their next target.

Through the clear dome of the *Poseidon*, the planet, small and blue at first, began to grow larger, and they could see the fine, exquisite details of a new world. It was familiar, comforting, and promising.

"The readout on my scanner looks good. There's oxygen down there breathable for humans." Kim said.

The blue planet looked a lot like Earth. Mac could see continents and blue oceans. There were vast mountain ranges, and as they got closer, he felt sure they were in the right place. The corbamite plate displayed the movie of a large field and three travelers crossing it on a sunny day. "Those are the wolf men I saw when the General first approached me about this trip. I believe we're here."

CHAPTER 7

THE POSEIDON NEARED THE BLUE planet. Mac thought that if this were the life-sustaining haven they hoped for when leaving Earth, and they could accomplish their mission, Neal's sacrifice would not have been in vain. Mac had been attempting to push out the images of Neal and the roaches eating him, but it was like a bad movie on repeat, as he sat watching the beautiful blue planet grow larger. He could see mountain ranges and rivers with more clarity. One vast continent stretched out in a charred black landscape, with volcanoes churning red-orange pools of lava so brilliant they could be seen from space. Grey clouds of smoke rose high into the sky as *Poseidon* neared the atmosphere. Mac had no rational explanation for the tightening in his stomach, but there was an ominous vibration emanating from the darkened, burning region of the planet. Mac steered them to the east toward a giant continent ringed with mountain ranges and forests.

"Here we go," Kim said. The crew was filled with nervous excitement.

The *Poseidon* soared through the atmosphere of this lush new planet, above green valleys, and over snow-covered mountain peaks. What the star travelers from earth did not know was that at the top of one peak they passed lived an ancient ice giant named Krill the Mongrel. As he watched the stranger's fly overhead, he growled at the silent craft and tossed a ten-foot-long ice javelin into the air at them. As the large metal disk whisked by Krill's mountain, Stephanie saw the ice rocket shoot harmlessly by.

"Did anyone else see that chunk of ice fly by us? Tell me I'm not the only one." Stephanie said. "Maybe it was a weather condition or something? We don't know what this planet's gravitational situation is. It's possible you saw ice in the clouds." Jack said.

"I think I'd know ice in the clouds when I saw it," Stephanie said.

"Sorry ma'am, I'm just here to work security," Jack said. He grinned and turned back in his chair to watch their descent.

A large white pyramid reaching for the heavens reflected the late-day sun, and below it, two more were visible in a line. These megalithic structures were constructed outside the forest near a shimmering ocean.

A radiant, translucent capstone splits the sunlight into a rainbow.

"You see those pyramids?" Kim asked. "They look very familiar."

"Yeah, a little too much like the ones on the roach planet. Jack said.

"Apparently pyramids are a universal constant," Mac said.

"I see a forest ahead," Mac said. They whooshed over the treetops of the wooded land, and as they did, a young wolven warrior looked up, turned his head toward them and began to walk in their direction through the forest.

Mac could see beyond the woods to a field of open grass and experienced an immediate feeling of déjà vu. It washed over him as they hovered over the exact spot where, in the movie, on General Martin's corbamite platter, he'd seen the three wolf men back on Earth.

"You alright, Colonel?" Jack asked.

"Yeah, just a little tired, that's all. I know we're in the right place. Kim, what's your environmental scanner reading now?" Mac asked and knew the answer. The three landing gear legs extended from their craft as it hovered above the field.

"It all looks good to me. We should be able to breathe normally without helmets here." Kim said.

"OK, let's get out, but be careful if you see bugs, strange plants, or anything with three heads, and give a shout-out if you do. Also, stay close to the craft so that we can hop on and beat it out of here if we need to." Mac said.

Mac lowered the ramp, while the team armed themselves with rifles again. The sun was setting over the large prairie. Tall grass covered the field and was roughly knee-deep. The air was fresher than any of them had experienced, and it carried an almost intoxicating perfume of summer flowers. White clouds hovered overhead as the Zeta 1 star, this planet's sun, began to dip below the skyline, giving way to twin moons that had not been visible to the crew when they had descended to the planet's surface. Stars twinkled above them like a blanket of sparkling diamonds as the travelers enjoyed their first moments on the new planet.

"This is a beautiful place. I wish we had something like this back home." Stephanie said.

"This may be home if we can manage to make nice with the locals and not start an intergalactic war. Do you hear that, everyone? Do not start an intergalactic war." Mac said.

"I'm hungry, and we haven't eaten today, I'm pretty sure. Let's tap into those rations." Kim said. "Not a bad idea. Although it's pretty out here, I think we'll spend the night inside our ship. I won't be sure about this place until we step out into the light of a new day and can explore. Predators tend to stalk the nighttime." Mac said. He missed his kids, but even here, so far from Earth, he couldn't help but think of Carol and how much she would love the scenery of this field. "Damn, I miss you."

He said to himself.

"What's that Mac?" Jack asked. His eyebrows were raised.

"Nothing, I'm just tired from a long day," Mac said.

"I agree. You know, if I didn't already know better, his could be Earth." Jack replied.

The forest beyond the field was populated with some of the largest trees he had ever seen, so tall they would have rivaled the height and girth of the great sequoias. For a moment, in the stillness, among shadows, he saw a form move beyond the tree line.

"I think we're being watched," Mac whispered. "You see something out there?" Jack asked. He was looking through the magnifying sight on his rifle.

"I wouldn't go waving rifles around unless we know for a fact, we're in danger. The locals might be feeling us out, and if you appear to be hostile, we may not get off on the best foot." Mac said.

"Yes, sir," Jack said and lowered his rifle.

The crew took shelter in the *Poseidon* now that it was completely dark. Their clear view of the star-filled sky was magnificent as there were no city lights to interfere with the nightscape. They each ate their rations in exhausted silence. Mac brought out the cosmic portal, detaching the small credit card-sized control mechanism for the cosmic portal. He missed his children so much that he contemplated taking the device outside and pushing the button now. His crew watched him palm the remote control in his hand and wondered if he would do it, but Mac decided against it, and placed the control back on the metallic device, pushing it aside and going back to his own meal.

Unknown to the crew, Dante, the young wolven hunter observing them, sent to locate those who would come from the stars, was watching them from high up in the trees. The strange hairless people who exited the craft were a curiosity, and he wondered with quiet excitement if they may be the ones he was sent to find. He also knew that the centaurs had been sending patrols close to his woods and had been instigating small skirmishes with some of his own people as the centaurs widened their reach. Gregor, the village chief, shaman, and wise man, had also sent Dante out on patrol days ago to make sure the forest had not been breached by centaur warriors. So far, this was the most interesting thing he had seen, and in the morning, he would go down and initiate contact with the strangers. His experience had been that night was a bad time to approach strange people.

Listening to the breeze singing through the forest, he sat in a tree, contemplating the future. Before long, the twinkling stars displayed another night of heaven's brilliance above him. Around midnight he fell asleep listening to the cricket's chirp and dreamed of an inevitable war.

"Are we opening the cosmic portal tomorrow?" Stephanie asked. Mac cocked his head as if giving the question great thought.

"Let's scout out the area first, maybe see if there *are* some locals, and decide if we're dealing with a hostile environment. If we open that portal and an army of snakes or those damned cockroach things come swarming through, this mission will have been for nothing. Looks can be deceiving,

even though it looks like we landed in paradise." Mac said.

"I'm a just playing Devil's advocate here, but wouldn't it be better, from a security perspective, if we open the cosmic portal and got armed reinforcements from home before engaging the locals?" Jack asked.

"Who may be hostile to strangers," Kim said. "I see your point, but we need to make sure that we're not opening the cosmic portal back to Earth and allowing a division of ET stormtroopers or something like that back to our home planet. I know we're kind of hanging out in the breeze here, but let's wait until we're reasonably sure that we're not dealing with hostiles, and then we can consider opening the gate. I also need to make sure none of us are going to drop dead from some microscopic biological bug native to this planet. Three days should give us time to burn in here. Let's see if we all live and then I give the all clear." "Strangers in a strange land," Stephanie said.

"I agree with the Colonel; waiting a few days is a great idea. We have no idea what kind of viruses are here." Kim said.

"It sounds like we're setting ourselves up for failure," Jack asked.

"How much worse would things be if this environment is poison, and we bring the last of the humans over here?" Kim replied.

"We'd be talking mass extinction. The end of the human race." Stephanie said.

"I still think we should protect ourselves with the rifles over there and if it seems like this is going south, we get the heck out of here," Jack replied. "I'm exhausted, let's eat and crash. Tomorrow's going to be a big day."

An hour later, the inflatable portable beds were set up, and all aboard were sleeping soundly. A chorus of snores filled the air as their first night on the new planet passed. As they slept, each of them dreamed of a wolf man in a robe, sitting around a ceremonial fire. He convened with them, candles burning in a circle around him as incense floated about his head like a cloud. He was in a state of deep meditation.

Then they could see the inside of an ancient library, the shelves filled with leather-bound books containing recipes, magical elixirs, and potions to alleviate all manner of maladies. The man was communicating with them in their dreams, and as he did, they could see a village of wolf men standing with outstretched arms and friendly smiling faces. His people would not harm the humans, and each party member felt a peaceful feeling of love as the shaman opened his eyes and smiled a large toothy grin.

Jack woke up with a full bladder, and the early morning sun shone in his eyes as his teammates slumbered. He rose from his bed and walked to the ramp, which descended at his arrival. He walked down, stopped halfway, and turned around to walk back up the ramp, lifting the surprisingly light cosmic portal and control unit, taking it outside with him. He took one of the rifles with him and lay it at the beside the ship as he unzipped the fly in his flight suit and relieved his bladder. Early morning dew clung to the grass, and the sun was not yet full height.

After relieving himself, Jack turned his attention to the cosmic portal. He had been curious about the device, and since his commander was asleep, he wondered if it could hurt to poke around with it. He also did not trust this new land and felt an urgency to open the gate so the human military could come through and secure the area. Before they left, the General had given him direct orders to open the cosmic portal as soon as possible when they landed on the right planet.

"Jack, I don't think I have to tell you how important this mission is, do I? You guys are it, because this is the only ET craft we have that's in one piece, and there are no more cosmic portals." General Martin said.

"Yes sir, I copy. You want me to get the gate open ASAP and get our troops through before someone out there figures out what we've got and tries to take it."

"That's correct lieutenant. You do this for me, and you'll jump two ranks. Major Sparling has a nice ring, doesn't it? Now, I want you to look for anything of material value that we can use when we rebuild over there. I'm talking about gold, diamonds, platinum, and precious metals. We need to establish another hierarchy of power and do it quickly."

"Yes, sir."

"We just can't have people running around uncontrolled over there when we repopulate, Sparling," the General said.

That had been their last conversation before Jack left. Now he was millions of light years from Earth, yet so close he could get home with the click of a button if he could figure out how it worked before Mac woke up. As he was hovering over the device, Jack heard hooves beating on the ground, as if someone on horseback were fast approaching. His mind turned to his gun, which was several yards from him.

"What are you and what are you doing?" A gruff male voice said from behind him. Jack's skin prickled at the sound as he turned.

"I'm a human from Earth and here on a peace mission," Jack said. Terror stole his voice when he turned to see three centaur warriors standing before him.

Each of the centaurs was eight feet in height with rippling biceps, bodies like that of mighty warhorses on legs like tree trunks, and strong hands that gripped menacing steel tridents. Jack swallowed hard, staring breathlessly into the face of a thickly bearded green man with slanted eyes, sharp horns protruding from his prominent forehead, and a long black mane of hair draping down his back. The lead centaur was frowning and had his trident raised for a strike when one of the centaurs in the back walked forward.

"I'm Yawl, General to Ragnok, King of the centaurs." He spoke. Yawl regarded Jack the same way a child with a magnifying glass looks at a bug he is about to fry with the sun. "Are there any more of you?" Yawl asked.

"I'm the only one," Jack answered.

Jack became more nervous now and knew that if he told this man what the cosmic portal could do, the centaurs would kill all of them and use the device to do God only knew what.

"What is that metal box behind you? Some sort of weapon?" Yawl asked.

"This is just a box filled with parts for the ship. I have to fix a gear so I can take off again." Jack said.

"He's lying," Lonas said.

Jack had dropped the remote control on the ground before he'd turned around, and he was scanning his memory to remember where it was now without looking down. Yawl was impatient and rose on his back legs in a show of force. When he did, Jack stumbled backward and landed hard on the remote with his rear end.

As he did, the rectangular metal artifact began to glow as rings of golden light formed from it in mid-air. The centaurs backed up a step as a dark portal filled in the opening inside the golden energy rings, and a trail through space rushed forward until it opened on the other end, inside a secret underground hangar where three maintenance men in jumpsuits got the surprise of their lives. They were looking at a hole in the west wall where three mythical figures from fairytale legends stared at them menacingly. They stopped what they were doing and stared with open mouths at the foreign world before them.

Dave, the shift supervisor, waved at them in shock as the portal began to close.

Jack rolled off the remote and grabbed it as Stephanie walked down the ramp, yawning. She had heard nothing of the commotion and was the second person awake. When she saw that Jack was missing, she decided to look for him. Stephanie got up and walked outside to see the portal closing and centaurs looming over Jack on the ground. Jack jumped up and ran toward her. The cosmic portal was now completely closed. When Jack darted up the ramp, Yawl tossed his trident through the air, hitting Jack in the center of his back with a loud *thump*, crushing his spine.

A crimson stream splattered Stephanie's flight suit as she stood horrified and confused. She shrieked. The three-pronged weapon stuck out of his chest as Jack fell to his knees, gasping for breath. The weight of the pole pulled him backward down the ramp and then caught him on the ground, propping him up like a deranged, bloody scarecrow. Jack was gurgling blood and wheezing; a sucking sound came from his chest as he raised his head to look at Stephanie. His mouth was filling with blood as he tried in desperate last attempt to warn

Stephanie to run, but it was too late, and he died propped up on his knees, staring into the new day sun.

From the left, Dante sprung through the air, punching Yawl in the mouth. Stephanie screams in terror.

"This does not concern you, wolven!" Yawl shouted.

"These are our lands, Yawl!

"I..I..I" Stephanie stammered. Her terror welled.

Yawl looked at one of his soldiers. "Take care of Dante, Petro!"

"Yes, sir!" Petro exclaimed

"Lonas, take the box!" Yawl yelled. Lonas galloped forward and swooped down, lifting the cosmic portal with ease.

Petro reared back and kicked Dante in the chest, knocking him to the ground. Dante sprang to his feet quickly, claws out, canines bared and charged Petro.

Before Stephanie could run away, she was in Yawl's powerful arms, struggling to get away. He held her under his pungent right armpit and began to trot away from the *Poseidon*. Stephanie screamed as they moved west toward the forest.

Mac was awakened by the commotion outside and jumped to his feet as he watched a trio of horsemen carrying Stephanie off through the spacecraft dome, now galloping at high speed. He grabbed his rifle and ran to the ramp, where he stopped. Before him was the deceased Jack Sparling, kneeling with a trident sticking out of his chest, arms flayed back, and facing the sky as if he were having a religious experience. Mac had two dead crew members on his conscience now. He ran past Jack, and when he reached the ramp's bottom, he raised his rifle.

Kim ran down after him. "Shoot the green guy; I saw those things kill Jack."

Mac aimed at Petro, firing his plasma rifle, and destroying his right front leg at the knee. Dante swiped the hobbled centaur across his throat with his sharp claws. Petro staggered around, choking as blood spilled from the wound in his neck. Mac fired again, hitting him in the shoulder, and Petro dropped to the ground, dead.

"What are you? Invaders from the sky?" Dante growled. He was seething with battle rage.

Mac turned to see the much larger wolfman walking toward him. He turned the barrel of his gun, sweating, and the beating of his heart grew louder in his ears. An eight-foot-tall nightmare of teeth and claws stood three feet away with a crossbow slung across his back. The wolf man's hazel-colored eyes held Mac with a fierce, penetrating gaze that made the Earthman feel as if his actions in the next few minutes could mean life or death in this strange new world.

"We're humans. I'm Colonel Mac MacDonald, and that's Lieutenant Kim Cross. They took one of our people. Can you help?" Mac said. He wiped a bead of sweat from his forehead.

Dante looked West. Yawl and Lonas had not yet reached the tree line. Dante gave Mac another suspicious glance and then ran after the centaurs. Dante caught up to Lonas, and as he dived through the air, the centaur turned with lightning speed on Dante, striking him in the chin with his trident. Dante fell to the ground unconscious. Lonas stops and looks down intently at an ornate dagger attached to Dante's belt.

"Yawl! Look what he has on him!" Lonas yelled.

"Take it, and let's get out of here before more of them show up!" Yawl yelled.

Lonas leaned down and ripped Dante's belt off, taking the dagger out of the sheath and tossing the belt on Dante's body. The two of them turn and vanish into the woods.

Mac walks over; his rifle held ready. "Hey, big guy! Wake up!" Mac yelled.

Dante's eyes pop open, and he jumped to his feet, feeling for his belt, and spots it lying on the ground "They took the shadow blade," Dante said. His head was bowed in frustration as he rubbed his bleeding chin.

"Thank you for your help, but I have to get that woman back. She's part of my crew and our only doctor." Mac said.

Dante brushes himself off.

"There's the thing. I also need to retrieve that dagger they stole, so it seems we may be able to help each other." Dante said.

Dante looks down at Mac. "Why would the centaurs want your metal box and woman?"

"Excellent! We have to get that back, too!" They begin walking back toward the ship as Kim joins them.

"We go after them, Colonel? You're not letting Stephanie go, are you?" Kim asked.

Mac crooks a thumb over his shoulder.

"No, but those jerks not only took Captain Brandt, but they also stole the cosmic portal, and this guy's knife," Mac said.

Kim stops in front of Dante and looks up. "Thank you for your help," Kim said.

"Don't mention it. I'm Dante of the Wolven tribe Blood Paw. I was watching your craft last night and fell asleep until Yawl and his cronies woke me up." Dante said.

Dante's gazed to the West thoughtfully for a moment.

"Welcome to Eritria, I've got to get that dagger back, but we'll need help. Where those centaurs are headed is dangerous territory.

"We really need to get that metal box back, right now. Can we follow the two who got away?" Mac asked.

"If you want to take on the entire centaur army, be my guest. I'm headed to my village to get help." Dante said.

Mac looks with increased impatience at the forest "How long's that going to take? What was Jack doing out here?"

Denat ignores him and walks in silence. Dante, Mac, and Kim return to the ship, and Kim kneels to pick something small and metallic out of the grass. It's the controller of the cosmic portal.

"They won't be able to open it without this.

Thank God." Kim exclaimed.

Kim handed Mac the controller, and he placed it inside a pocket of his flight suit. Without a word, Dante walked over to Jack and dragged his body out to the open field.

"What are you doing?" Mac asked.

Dante produced a small leather pouch from the bag attached to his hip and walked over to where Jack's body lay. He reached inside the pouch with two of his fingers and produced a white powder that he sprinkled on Jack's body. He was muttering something, but Kim and Mac could not make sense of it. He stepped back, and in an instant, green flames engulfed the dead man, emulsifying him down to the skeleton. In a few more minutes even his skeletal frame had vanished.

"Predators would have eaten your friend by sundown," Dante said.

"Thank you for...taking care of our friend," Mac said.

"You're welcome. We can't leave bodies lying around out here, so as soon as someone's soul moves on to the next world, we burn them. Certain unscrupulous necromancers have also raised our own dead against us in times past." "Hold on, like zombies or something? People here can do that?" Kim asked.

Dante nods.

"That metal box is our way home, and we must get it back before anything happens to it," Mac said.

Mac turned toward the star craft and slid his hand over a metallic hieroglyphic on the side of the ship, and the ramp ascended. Kim had taken two rifles from their supplies, handed one to Mac, and then they followed Dante east into the woods.

"What were those things that took Stephanie?" Mac asked.

"Centaurs and I don't know what they were doing this far into our hunting grounds, but I suspect they're planning another war with us," Dante said.

"War?" Mac asked.

"You think they're testing their boundaries?" Kim asked.

"Yes, I do. A long-time armistice between our races is crumbling. The centaurs are definitely testing the borders."

"Feeling you out?" Mac asked.

Dante nodded. "Exactly. War is looming Mac from Earth." Dante said.

His voice came out as a growl that raised the hair on Mac's neck, giving him cold shivers. They all walked on in silence while Mac thought about the smiling faces of his children and wondered if he would ever see them again.

CHAPTER 8

AS THEY WALKED ALONG A dirt path through the forest, Mac thought of Stephanie and wondered if she was still alive. He thought of Stephanie's daughter nine light years away, awaiting her mother's reappearance, ignorant of the possibility that she may never see her again.

Long dark shadows fell like demonic fingers through the deep forest as sunlight fought through the thick canopy above. The forest was alive with the screeching mating calls of birds and buzzing of insects as the trio marched toward Dante's village. They were pursued by biting mosquitoes and small creatures flitting about their faces.

"Darned gnats!" Mac barked.

"Those are most likely sprites. Dangerous if angered." Dante said.

"Sprites?" Mac asked. With each new revelation from Dante, Mac only had more questions.

The forest opened to a clearing with a convergence of four paths, each one winding its way through the trees in different directions. There were four wooden road signs crafted in the shape of directional arrows; words were etched upon them with a fine instrument. They were pointing each direction of the compass and written on them were the words *North to Draxford, West to the Open Plains and Bog Lands, South to the Fairy Lands, and East to Wasatch Village.*

"Gregor will be pleased to see you. My father has been waiting a long time for your ship to fall out of our sky." Dante said.

"You knew we would be coming," Mac said. "Gregor did, yes. Our shaman, with the aid of powerful mushrooms, travel astrally to other dimensions, and if their mind is strong enough, they are shown what may be in the past, present, and future." Dante said.

"And your father saw all of this?" Mac asked. "No, one of my ancestors did several hundred years ago. Biminium witnessed a blue planet far from here, her people in grave danger of extinction, seeking another world."

"But why are the centaurs your enemy?" Mac asked.

"Did you see those pyramids behind our village?" Dante asked.

"On the way in, yes."

"Those pyramids and the forest you are standing in were once the kingdom of Malduk the Invincible. Wolvacar." Dante said.

Mac looked around and saw the remnants of stone walls, obscured by thick, choking foliage in the forest.

"In those days, all five clans were under the rule of Malduk. Our people were the guardians of the light and caretakers of this land."

"OK," Mac said.

"Ragnok and the Faerie King Ardeuceus laid siege to Wolvacar in an effort to gain control of the pyramids."

"Why would they do that?" Kim asked.

"The pyramids were the MOST powerful machines on this continent, capable of producing enormous, endless natural energy. Ardeuceus and Ragnok desired their power for evil purposes. The initial battle raged for over a week, with a stalemate on both sides. A massive stone wall stood where Wasatch Woods ends, blocking their ingress, but then..." Dante stopped talking.

"Then?" Mac asked.

"Tens of thousands of Ragnok's centaur and faerie warriors, warlocks, and mages lay strewn about the battlefield. He could not breach Malduk's defenses until his men dug under the wall and blew a large hole in the side of it. Wolven were forced to repel a swarm of incoming enemies, and as the fighting moved beyond the wall, Malduk's mages were able to cast a barrier spell over the gash, but not before hundreds of wolven were trapped on the outside, slaughtered by Ragnok and Ardeuceus. That is when centaur warlocks brought the dead wolven back from the grave to fight against their own people. Ragnok began launching the undead over the wall on catapults. These were mindless savages bereft of souls, bent on destruction. The undead destroyed a totem left at the wall breach, and when that went down, the enemy streamed in. Wolvacar was overrun and almost defeated. Malduk was forced backward toward the pyramids with one of his mages, Terrel."

"They used the pyramids against the army, right?" Kim asked.

"Indeed. None but the king himself could activate the power within those devices. A smaller pyramid on a pedestal stood just outside the Great Pyramid. Malduk removed an amulet from around his neck and placed it inside the small pyramid. When he did this, a massive discharge of energy passed from the pyramid to the obelisks, destroying most of the invading army and taking Wolvacar down with it. Our once proud city was destroyed, and countless wolven slaughtered in the energy blast."

"Total war," Mac said.

"Yes, and because of this, when the war was over, and Ragnok retreated, Malduk's Generals lost faith in his leadership, save for my father, who eventually became our new leader. That is how the five tribes were created, and although we have not been to war with the centaurs in over three hundred years, they are an ever-present threat."

"That's an incredible tale," Kim said. "It certainly was brutal," Mac said.

Mac thought for a moment about his encounter with Jack that morning as he ran down the ramp of their ship. His mind's eye saw the frozen death mask on Jack's face and watched his gaping mouth twist out the words, "Why did you let this happen to me?"

"If you had been doing your job, you'd be alive," Mac whispered.

"What's that, sir?" Kim asked. "Nothing, sorry, just talking to myself."

He felt a strong desire to turn around and hunt down the centaurs on his own, but with conscious effort, Mac put the death of Jack and Neal to the back of his mind and concentrated his thoughts on Bobby and Serena instead. He was going to get that cosmic portal back if he had to gun down an army of centaurs; his kids were counting on him to succeed.

"I'm sorry about your friends, the man murdered by Yawl and the female that was taken, but you must have something Yawl wants, or they would have killed her already. Centaurs give no quarter to their enemies."

"That's comforting," Mac said.

"You know, Gregor described your craft in his visions. He said it would be a disc shape and come from the clouds, so when I saw you coming from out of the sky, I decided to follow your ship just in case. I almost couldn't believe it myself, but there you were." Dante said.

Mac began to feel the reality of their new situation sinking in. He was millions of miles from home, no more people from Earth with them, and he was walking through the woods with a giant talking werewolf. They were now on a quest to meet his tribe. Mac took a deep breath and looked at Kim, who expressed uncertainty similarly. He suddenly wanted to sit down for a moment as the stress of their day swept over him.

"How far is your village, Dante?" Mac asked. "At this pace, two days, why?" Dante said. "Just curious. One second, I've got a rock in my boot." Mac replied.

A small black cloud of winged creatures flitted about Mac's face. He waved at them, striking a few with his hand as he walked toward a two-foot- tall rock to sit on.

"Gnats!" Mac said.

To his left, a larger rock surrounded by tall grass stuck out of the ground. The black cloud of creatures formed a small orb, and as Mac sat down, a bolt of energy erupted from within it, aimed at him. As he moved, the bolt missed Mac and struck the boulder.

"You there, what are you doing?!" Said an old woman's voice.

"What?" Mac said.

"Well, you're on my head and had better get off before I bite you on the behind!" The voice was angry.

He looked down to see two hollowed-out eyes looking up at him and a horizontal crack opening in a scowl.

"Aaaagh! What the..." Mac shouted.

He hopped off the rock with lightning speed, slamming his head into a tree beside him. Mac hit the ground and was knocked unconscious by a very cross rock who frowned, grumbled for a moment, and then went back to sleep. When Mac woke up a few minutes later, he rested below a tree with a bough of soft leaves under his head. Inside his mouth was the taste of sulfur, garbage, or something else, and he spat a wad of brown sludge onto the ground.

"Ugh, that's gross. Sorry, I must have fallen asleep." Mac said. He was groggy and slurring his speech. Little bugs had been using his face as a landing strip since he hit the ground and headed for friendlier ground when he stirred.

"Fallen asleep? You slammed your head into that tree you're sitting under, Mac. That rock over there barked at you, and then you smashed your head." Kim said.

"I tried to warn you about the sprites. I put some cama herbs in your mouth to stave off a concussion." Dante said.

"It was nice to have some downtime," Kim said.

A large black bird swooped down from the top of a nearby tree, startling Mac, and Kim. She was larger than an ostrich, and her onyx feathers shimmered in the morning sun as she disappeared behind a pile of fallen trees in the brush. A moment later, there was rustling in the leaves, some grunts, and then the bird was flapping her powerful wings again, rising above the rotting pile of trees. In her talons was a pig-like creature about the size of a mule. The beast squealed and thrashed in the talons of his more powerful adversary, realizing he was trapped, but refusing to submit. The giant bird gave a triumphant squawk and vanished above the treetops carrying her prey, leaving the trio in silence once more. "What was that?" Mac asked. His eyes were wide as saucers.

"I've never seen a bird that big before," Kim said.

"That was a narand hawk, and her prey, a kiney."

"The trees in this forest are massive," Kim said "Good shade and protection from enemies. These woods are so thick in places that if you get lost, you might never find your way out. Skeletons litter the ground from travelers who divert from the road and wander too far. Wasatch Forest's trees protect us from harsh weather and hide our homes from danger." Dante said.

The three had been walking uphill for some time, brushing against tall ferns and rhododendron trees, when the sound of rushing water and a struggle could be heard. Dante sniffed the air.

"What?" Mac asked.

"Shhhh," Dante said and walked toward the river.

He crept down toward the sound of rushing water, while Mac and Kim checked their weapons. Mac motioned for Kim to follow him and raised his plasma rifle to ready. They stayed within a safe distance of their host, never letting him out of their sight. They stopped about fifty feet from Dante as he gazed through the trees, and Mac could not see further. Dante looked back at the two earthlings and motioned for them to join him. When Mac and Kim reached him, Dante put a finger in front of his mouth for them to remain quiet and pointed to the water.

Thirty yards from their vantage point, milling about in the water, were six five-foot-tall porcupine men who seemed to be hunting something below the surface. Draped down their backs were three-foot-long quills. They were growling at each other in a language that Mac could not understand.

"Libmok's," Dante whispered. "Very dangerous, let's go. We'll get water further up the stream."

Dante was turning around to go when they saw the head of a tiny man resembling a mole and no taller than three feet pop his head above the water and gasp for air.

"A mole man?" Mac said.

Dante's turned back, eyes widening, and he bared his teeth.

"Rasp!" Dante yelped.

The libmok's descended upon the little man as Dante pulled the crossbow from off his back and knocked a bolt. He fired into the crowd, dropping one of them into the rushing water as his bolt ripped between the quills and severed the libmok's spine. He knocked another bolt and sprung from his hiding place, running toward the surprised porcupine men.

"What are you waiting for?! Come on!" Dante yelled at the humans.

Dante fired again toward the five remaining libmok's, but this time his shot went wide, and he missed. They turned on him and scowled, their quills sticking out in wide fans across their backs as they each pulled a quill free, holding them outstretched toward Dante, like a fencing foil. The tiny forgotten mole man swam away from his attackers to the other bank. Mac was not sure exactly what was going on, but he knew Dante was probably his only chance to get Stephanie and the cosmic portal back, so he knew it was in his best interest to help.

He raised his rifle and fired a round at the libmok closest to Dante, marveling at the cannonball-sized hole that opened in the creature's chest. The libmok barked a cry of protest and fell dead on his face into the water.

"Watch the quills; they're filled with a deadly poison that kills within hours of contact. Our people have formed immunity to the venom, but you may not be so fortunate." Dante said.

He rushed forward, his claws like knives at the tips of his fingers, and dived under their quill swords with expert movement, impaling two of the libmok's through their midsections. As he lifted them high over his head, one of the libmok's lunged forward with his quill and nearly caught Dante in the ribs. Had it not been for the quick reflexes of Kim Cross, he would have been stabbed. She fired a plasma round at the libmok, erasing its hand in a spray of green blood and bone splinters. It let out an earsplitting bellow as the quill that had almost pierced Dante dropped to the ground at his feet.

Kim fired again, and this time she knocked the libmok to his knees. The creature died a moment later, floating downstream, face staring up at the clear sky. Dante held his two libmok's aloft with iron strength as if they were deranged hand puppets, and then easily tossed them like cordwood into the flowing water. The remaining libmok turned on Mac, and as the colonel was aiming to fire another burst of plasma, the libmok chucked his quill like a javelin. As the round left his rifle, the tip of the quill went deep into Mac's right leg, and the head of the offending libmok exploded like a pumpkin dropped from the top of a tall building.

Mac gave him a confused look, muttering, "It hit me," and stumbled once as he tried to walk, and then fell unconscious to the ground.

"The tiny mole man on the other side ran into the thick undergrowth. "That little man is running away!" Kim screamed.

"Mole men are our friends, and Rasp was returning from a mission for my father in Moktar.

We have to get Mac to Wasatch village before Mac dies from this venom." Dante said. "Climb on my back." He spoke.

Dante knelt and ripped a sleeve from Mac's flight suit. He tied the sleeve around Mac's leg, above the wound, to slow the poison, and picked up the unconscious, dying earthman as Kim climbed onto his back. She felt the rippling muscles of Dante's back running across his shoulders and back as her hands got a good hold. *This man is enormous*, she thought. When Kim had wrapped her arms around him, Dante stood and ran through the forest.

In an hour they reached a clearing and entered a log cabin village that reminded Kim of a small city. The houses were constructed with timber from the forest and blended in so well that if you were not looking, you might never see it. Kim could not remember having seen the town from above as they flew over.

Dante created a stir as passing wolven stopped and turned to see the oddity he carried in his arms and the one on his back. Kim could see the tops of the pyramids far from town, rising above the trees. There were three of them she could see, the two smallest were red and black, but the largest pyramid was ivory white and reflected the sun like a brilliant land-based star. Her mood was suddenly lighter as she looked at it and Dante drew closer. There was some kind of spiritual energy coming from those structures, and she began to weep with an overwhelming sense of happiness. The charge coursed through her body like an electrical storm, lessening her care and worry.

Kim shook her head and looked around at the modern houses, shops, apartment buildings and streets lined with cobblestones. She felt as if she had been transported to a wealthy pioneering town from the 1800s in America, but the large scale and depth of this city were unparalleled. Dante had misled them when he used the term village, Kim thought. He ran with them to a large house at the end of a cul-de-sac. This house was of log and stone construction like the rest but had prismatic crystals hanging from the porch and the strong odor of patchouli drifting out to greet them. The scent was so strong that it managed to escape through a closed wooden door and invade Kim's nostrils like an advancing army. Dante ran up the stairs and burst through the door.

"Father, we need your help. This human was poisoned with libmok venom!" Dante said.

Gregor stood in his kitchen fixing a pot of tea as the door banged open. "Humans in Eritria? We have little time; the poison has reached his temples. Take him into the guest quarters." Gregor said.

"Right away!" Dante growled.

"The prophecy has come to pass. Rasp just left here with news of a possible coming war with the centaurs." Gregor said.

At that moment, another wolven entered the room, Ramos, Dante's brother. He wore a black leather vest, sported earrings along his left ear and tattoos on his shoulders.

"What are these?" Ramos asked. "Humans, from Earth," Dante said.

"Oh, here to complete the prophecy?" Ramos said.

Dante shrugged. "So far, they've only caused trouble."

"Can you save him?" Kim said, her voice frantic.

"I will do what I can," Gregor said.

"Gregor will help Mac. His magic is strong." Dante said.

"I hope so. I don't want to do this alone," Kim said.

"I have to drain the poison; go get my kit!" Gregor barked.

"Yes, Father," Dante said and vanished into the other room.

"The venom is potent, and my blood may kill him, but he's dead if we do nothing.

He took Mac into an adjacent room off the living room, and a moment later, they were joined by a smaller, hunched, wolven man in a maroon robe. He wore silver and gold earrings with a solid gold hoop through his nose. His robe had been woven with gold thread and decorated with planets and stars. As he passed by her, Kim could see that one of the planets on the back of his robe resembled Earth with such exactness that it could have been a photograph of her home planet.

"Father, these humans landed in the plains outside Wasatch Forest. One of them, a woman, was kidnapped, the other killed by centaurs, and this one was stabbed by a libmok quill when we rescued Rasp from a group of them in the sandy creek." Dante said.

Gregor grinned at Kim with a toothy smile.

Dante came back into the room holding some clear, flexible tubing and a small wooden box that, when opened, revealed two medium-sized steel needles.

"A blood transfusion," Kim whispered. Gregor took the needles out and connected them to the tubes. One end went into Mac's right arm, and the other needle was inserted into Gregor's left.

"What's your name, child?" Gregor asked. "I'm Kim Cross, the team science officer, and that's Colonel MacDonald, Mac. He's our commander. Our medical officer, Stephanie Brandt, was kidnapped by a centaur named Yawl." Kim said. Her words felt strange as she described their experience.

"He and his men stole our cosmic portal."

Mac was moaning as the veins in his neck turned a dark, sickly green under the skin; the libmok's' poison was working through his circulatory system so fast now that they could see it moving toward his brain, like the tendrils of a monster inside his flesh.

"Welcome to Eritria, Kim," Gregor said. He was seated beside Mac as his side of the flexible line slowly replaced the poison in Mac's blood.

"Turn around," Gregor said. "That's us?" Kim asked.

There was a mural etched in wood, depicting several scenes in four separate quadrants. The first quadrant showed a disk-shaped craft with a dead humanoid man on the ground just in front of its ramp, and centaurs standing over him with a rectangular device in one of their hands, while another centaur had a smaller figure from the craft slung across his back. In Quadrant Two, two humans enter the village of Wolven. In quadrant three, in the lower left-hand corner, the humanoids and an army of wolven and Minotaur were beset on all sides by an army in battle. In the fourth quadrant, the most interesting, Kim could see the humanoids standing before a great ring of light and the front of a modern-looking earth vehicle coming through.

"What happened?" Gregor asked. His eyes met Kim's, and his fuzzy brow was furrowed.

"Dante was helping a little furry man get away from those libmok things down by this river, and we had killed almost all of them when Mac was hit with a quill," Kim said.

"You'd planned to use this cosmic portal to open a doorway to your dying planet, correct?" Gregor said. Mac was beginning to stir, and the beads of sweat that had broken out on his forehead were drying.

"How did you know that?" Kim said.

"Let me show you something," Gregor said, pointing to the wall behind her. Mac opened his eyes and grunted as Kim turned around.

"Oh my god, that's us?" Kim asked.

"That was carved three hundred years ago by my uncle Biminum when he went into a trance one afternoon," Gregor said.

"What was in that drink?" Mac grumbled. "You're awake. The transfusion worked; you had me worried for a moment." Gregor said.

"I saw that same wood carving in my dream...and a great war," Mac said.

"Your arrival here was not by chance, my friends. My name is Gregor. I am the chief and medicine man of this village." Gregor removed the needle from his arm and the one from Mac's and placed a small bandage on each puncture mark as Mac sat up slowly on the elbow of his good arm. "Is that us?"

"You tell me. Who else could it be? I admit, I was skeptical I'd see the prophecy fulfilled in my lifetime, but now I realize the time has come." Gregor said.

"I feel strange," Mac said.

His head was swimming with the poison, but there was something else as well, a sort of anxious anticipation and restlessness.

"You may for a while. My blood is inside you right now, and it's a miracle that you survived the transfusion," Gregor said.

"Will it pass?" Mac asked. "I don't know."

"We have to get our friend back, Gregor. They also took our cosmic portal; luckily, they can't operate it without this." Mac said. He pulled the controller out of his pocket and waved it in the air. "Lonas also knocked me unconscious, and Ragnok stole the Shadow Dagger," Dante said. "He did what?!" Gregor growled.

"You're in trouble now, brother," Ramos smirked.

"How could you be so irresponsible? Does anyone else know?" Gregor asked. He shook his head in frustration and anger.

"The one thing we're never supposed to touch, and you lose it. Nice going." Ramos said. "Ramos, that is quite enough. Dante, why did you remove it from the vault?" Gregor asked.

"I don't remember doing it, father!" Dante yelled.

"We've only been told a million times to leave that dagger alone. Good job, little brother." Ramos chided.

"Ramos, enough!" Gregor yelled.

"The council will hang you for this," Ramos said.

"No, they won't, because we're going to get it back before word spreads. Why, Dante?" Gregor said.

"I wish I knew, father. I don't remember taking it, but just before Lonas hit me, I realized the dagger was on my hip." Dante said.

"Probably not my place to ask, but what's the deal with that dagger?" Mac asked.

"After the defeat of his army, Ardeuceus, king of the fairies, ordered the execution of Malduk. Malduk got word of this and laid siege to his castle with what remained of his army of wolven and minotaur." Gregor started.

"Malduk's forces broke through the faerie defenses, and he made his way to the underground vault, where

Malduk found the source of their power, a large, dark blue crystal." Ramos continued.

"Ardeuceus followed him, and the two had a tremendous fight, but Malduk was the more powerful warrior and managed to shatter the crystal," Gregor said.

"Without the crystal, the faeries were powerless, and when Malduk stuck the blade into King Ardeuceus, killing him, their souls entered the dagger, trapped within it to this day," Ramos said.

"So, what's the problem? I still don't understand." Mac said.

"Not all the faeries were killed; many escaped and have not been seen since. But one day, a traveling warlock came to Wasatch village and told of a massive statue erected on the faerie lands' border." Dante said.

"A magnificent lion constructed of volcanic rock and the dust from that crystal. If the dagger touches that crystal, the faeries will return and wage war against the wolven again." Ramos said. "If the council of elders finds out about this, Dante will be hanged for treason," Gregor stated. "I am going to get it back, and since this would not have happened if the Earth people had not come here, Mac has agreed to help me, and I him,"

Dante said.

"The prophecy is unfolding, and all that happens henceforth was predicted long ago. You cannot blame the Earth people for that." Gregor said.

"Have you ever considered that the prophecy is superstitious nonsense and Biminium was an addled-minded fool?" Ramos asked.

Gregor growled at his mocking son. "Superstitious nonsense, or no, we have a dagger to retrieve, and these people need their cosmic portal. I'd focus on that if I were you." Gregor said.

He stood and stormed out of the house, slamming the door behind him. Mac looked at Dante and then Ramos, eyebrows raised.

"He'll be fine once he cools down. Dante, you stepped in it this time. Ha! What were you thinking?" Ramos said.

"I already told you what I know. Now, drop it, Ramos!" Dante said. He was standing with his claws out and furrowed brow.

"Mac, are you alright?" Kim asked. "Just a little dizzy."

"Probably father's blood. There's no telling what effect it'll have on you." Dante said. "Anyone hungry? I'm ravenous, and there's a steak special at the Grumpy Bear Inn." Ramos said. They all nodded, and after Kim helped Mac to his feet, the four of them walked out the door.

As the sun set, Dante and Ramos's shadows stretched along the ground, and to Mac, they looked like walking fur-covered buildings. They approached The Grumpy Bear Inn and entered, passing by a group of wolven men standing around the door. Their faces were crossed with suspicion as the humans followed close behind Dante.

"What's the matter? Have you never seen humans before? Mind your own business." Dante said. The men returned to their business without comment.

Mac thought it looked like Dante had serious sway over these people and felt more comfortable around him. The bar was crowded as they entered, and the men were drinking a tinted brown beverage from glass mugs. Dante led Mac and Kim to a table. "Rathgar! Four barberry juices, please!" Ramos yelled.

A beleaguered-looking wolven man who had been wiping down the bar looked over at Ramos and gave a big thumbs up. The drinks came minutes later from a shapely wolven woman with large breasts and a brown suede leather skirt. Mac felt a strange yearning for her, something oddly sexual.

"Hi, boys, who are your new friends? You two are THE talk of the town."

"Hello Shannon, they're humans from Earth. Mac here is on a mission to sleep with wolven women and forge a new race," Ramos said. Shannon laughed and caressed the back of Mac's head. "Honey, when you're ready to get wild, come see me," Shannon said, walking away.

"Take it easy on that liquor, my friend. It'll twist you." Dante said.

Mac nodded, took a sip, and smiled. "Whoa, this tastes like strawberries and peaches," Kim said.

"I feel like I just ate a big bag of psychedelic mushrooms," Mac said.

"I think he's had enough," Ramos said. "I can hear colors." Kim smiled.

"Her too," Dante replied.

A moment later, the door slammed open, and in walked a large black wolven man adorned with a skull necklace, silver earrings, and wrist bracers crafted with the broken teeth of what Mac could only guess had been this man's enemies. An ominous dread sunk deep into Mac's stomach as this frightening new stranger sauntered into the room, sneering.

Ramos' eyes narrowed and his fists clenched. "Double Head." He spoke.

CHAPTER 9

"**W**HERE ARE THE EARTHMEN?!" Double Head yelled, disrupting the bar. He looked around the room until he spotted the strangers. He pointed to Mac and glared at him with burning eyes.

Mac's frightened, tripping mind struggled to understand what was happening. He had been laughing and joking with his new friends only a minute ago and now seemed to be the target of a large, angry wolven.

He sat stone still, sweat beading on his forehead, and the flashback of a Doberman cornering him against a fence when he was little popped into his mind. Double Head stormed across the room, moving tables as he went, whether they had people sitting at them or not until he was standing over Mac with his claws bared and teeth showing. Mac knew whatever happened would change the outcome of his life dramatically.

"These humans are going to bring doom upon us all! We've got to get rid of them before they multiply!" Double Head barked.

Dante moved to stop Double Head, and the Chief punched him in the mouth. Then Double Head lifted Mac from his seat with one arm and tossed him behind the bar like a rag doll. He turned on Kim, but Ramos stood up and punched Double Head in the jaw, flipping the Chief's head to the side violently. Ramos and Dante then stood in front of Kim, guarding her against the enraged Double Head.

"What's gotten into you?! Go home to your tribe; these are not your woods, Chief!" Dante said.

Double Head threw an elbow into Dante's jaw that hit so hard, Dante's head knocked into his brother's.

"Hey!" Ramos barked.

"I'm gonna' knock your head off!" Dante yelled.

Just as the brothers were about to take on the larger, more battle-hardened warrior chief, they heard a gut-wrenching howl from behind the bar. It was so loud that all involved stopped and turned to see where it came from. Mac lay on the floor burning, screaming, twisting in pain as his legs elongated two feet and feral rage coursed through him.

Writhing in pain, he lay on the floor in the fetal position, his muscles expanding and tearing through old tissue. He felt the itch and the sharpening of teeth. His arms grew three times their size—bulging with massive, rippled muscles—and his face distorted the head of a wolven. White fur sprouted from his pores, and he bellowed in agony as Gregor's blood boiled within his own, changing him into something not quite human anymore. When the transformation was complete Mac was an eight-foot-tall wolven man standing in a bar where all eyes were wide and staring, including Double Head's. Several locals immediately made their way out the door, terrified of the cursed shapeshifter.

"Hey ugly! Why don't you try throwing me again?" Mac said, growling.

Mac leaped onto the bar with lightning speed and dived for Double Head, who had not been expecting the attack. Mac had long black claws now, and as he toppled his opponent, Mac dug his claws into Double Head's shoulders with a vicelike grip and then tore into his muscles as he screamed with rage. Double Head was pinned to the floor in a minute, taken off his base by the shock of this mutant's attack. He was suddenly terrified; he didn't know if Mac was a necromancer or some kind of warlock from another world.

"Get off me!" Double Head yelled, and kneed Mac in the stomach, knocking him backward into a wall of glasses, half of which shattered on the plank wood floor as they fell off the shelves.

"We have no quarrel with you!" Mac yelled and leaped forward. The chief stepped to the side, allowing Mac to run by, but not before the Colonel took a quick swipe on the way, cutting Double Head's face.

"You should leave while you still can, humans before you bring more damage than your arrival has already caused. There are other worlds to explore! So, go trouble their people." Double Head said.

Dante pulled Mac off Double Head, as Ramos grabbed his kicking legs. Mac howled with uncontrollable rage. Gregor was walking by the inn and heard the commotion from outside. Concerned by the sound of the violence, he burst through the door.

"Stop this right foolishness, right now!" Gregor growled.

Mac slowed his struggling, and Double Head lowered his claws, glancing back and forth between Gregor and Mac.

"Double Head, this is not your village. You have come to trade and accomplished your goal; you need to leave." Gregor growled.

"Gregor, this prophecy you have all been holding onto is going to be the downfall of our civilization." Double Head said.

"The prophecy has promised the end of Asura!" Gregor said.

"You've forgotten what tribe means because of your 300-year-old fantasy. These people from the stars have technology that can rip us apart!" Double Head said.

"Your superstition about the men from Earth is completely unfounded!" Gregor said.

"As is your prophecy of alien travelers as saviors! In *my* visions, I have seen the rain of fire and a giant mushroom in the sky! I'm begging you. You cannot continue down this path. Turn them away." Double Head said.

"In my visions, I have seen strange vehicles and weapons that belch flames aiding us in a final war against Asura. Nowhere in the prophecy is there a hint that the outsiders mean us harm." Gregor said.

"Suit yourself, but this will not turn out as you have foreseen. And now it appears one of them has become half-wolven." Double Head said. He was shaking his head as he walked toward the door.

"You are a fool." He said, and then he was gone into the night.

The barberry juice had been too much for him, and as Mac stumbled forward, noticing that even though his vision was more acute and his sense of smell was heightened, he was losing control and fell face-first to the floor. As he released his mind into unconsciousness, he began to feel like himself again. Dante and his brother looked closer and watched as he returned to his human form. Gregor calmed the bar down, and Ramos bought another two rounds for everyone in the room. Then Dante and Ramos carried the unconscious commander back to Gregor's house. There Mac would be safe just in case any of the tribe had ideas about killing Mac. Kim followed, and the two humans were given separate rooms adjoining one another.

"Are we in danger on Eritria, I mean, from your people? Why does Double Head think we've come to do you harm?" Kim asked.

"Double Head follows his visions with blind faith, as do we all because they are messages from our ancestors. I know the Blood Paw tribe will have to rely on Double Head's courage and that of his tribe when war comes, but in my visions, I have seen help from your people through great hardship, although it is not all clear. The visions are a lot like pieces of a puzzle." Gregor said.

The next morning Mac was sleeping off the effects of the barberry juice, his uniform lying in the corner, shredded to threads when he burst through it the night before. He dreamed of home, where Bobby and Serena were playing in the field by the old stricken tree, kicking a red ball back and forth, laughing without a care. The sun shone upon them as he watched, and he felt a pang of homesickness accompanied by a longing to reach out and touch them, but they were separated from him by a glass wall, a voyeur of his own life. Mac began to pound on the glass. He sensed someone to his left, and when he turned to look, a snow- white wolf man glared back at him. He felt the walls shake as the world around him tumbled into small pieces. Mac shot up in bed with a start. He was disoriented and confused.

"Where am I?" Mac whispered to himself.

The room was spinning, and his head pounded like a loud marching band was practicing between his eardrums. Mac had a vague recollection of some altercation with a wolven chief, where he landed violently behind a bar and blacked out. As he sat in bed, eyes shut tight, he saw gnashing teeth and long, sharp claws in his mind. He did not know what time it was precisely but knew the early morning was upon him as he looked out the window to see the day's first rays of the sun glowing through the tall pines. What had they been drinking last night?

Whatever they had fed him was strong and deadly serious. Bilbar juice? No, that wasn't right. Something juice, though. Mac got up and walked over to a mirror hanging on the wall, and for a moment, as if a ghost had passed before him, he saw the white wolven staring at him, and then it disappeared. He stumbled backward, tripping over an old chest at the foot of the bed, and landed hard on his bottom.

Suddenly, Mac remembered his missing crewmate. He knew he needed to get Stephanie back as soon as possible, with or without the tribe's help.

"You're up!" Gregor said. Mac turned and saw him standing in the doorway.

"Ugh, I feel like a bomb went off in my head, and an alligator crapped in my mouth," Mac said. "You should probably go slower on the barberry juice next time," Gregor said. "Although you certainly made an impression on Double Head."

"What happened to me?" Mac asked. "Something I've never seen before. It seems that when I gave you my blood, it merged with yours. And when you were thrown behind the bar by Double Head, you morphed wolven for a brief period of time." Gregor said.

"I what?! Is this a permanent thing? Am I going to turn again? Will I become completely wolven?" Mac asked, terrified.

"I'm sorry; I don't have any answers for you. Gregor said, lowering and shaking his head. "You fought Double Head and then passed out from the fermented juice. My boys carried you back here."

"Are we in danger, Gregor?" Mac asked.

"Not from us or Double Head's tribe for now. Things will calm down after a few days, but the most important thing for all of us is securing your crew members and cosmic portal, and that Shadow Blade before anyone else in the tribe discovers it is missing. " Gregor said.

"Can you tell me more about the prophecy?" Mac asked.

"When wolven shamans meditate, through the use of special herbs, the visions presented manifest in the physical realm. Our spirit guides show us what we need to see to grow and heal most of the time, but then there are other visions meant to warn our people of impending danger. I began to lose hope I would see the revelation in my lifetime, but it is coming. I know it like I sense the change in seasons."

Kim entered the room, wiping sleep from her eyes.

"That drink was evil, Gregor. I have to watch how much of that I have next time, and you sir, should never drink it again. That was quite a show you put on last night; it scared half the bar." Kim said.

Mac looked down with a small grin and rubbed his matted hair.

A knock came at the front door.

"That'll be Dante and Ramos. We'll eat some breakfast and be on our way. The rifles you came with are in my study leaning against the wall." Gregor opened the door, and Dante came over to Mac right away. Ramos was more reserved and stood by the door with their father shaking his head.

"Brother!" Dante hugged Mac.

The larger wolven grabbed him as an adult with a small child, shaking his smaller body like a doll, and if Mac had not begun to know these people, the experience would have been alarming at best. Mac could smell Dante's fur, which reminded him of his dog Sparx, which he had as a child just after bathing the animal. His fur smelled of chamomile and lavender mixed with canine musk, creating a nostalgic aroma that was not unpleasant but animalistic and endearing. Mac thought that Anything smelled better than Gregor's house's patchouli-laden aroma.

"That was quite a display last night, Mac. Most of the town is talking about it this morning." Ramos said.

"Any of it good?" Mac asked, wincing.

"Most of them think you're some kind of shape-shifting warlock or a demon sent here from another dimension," Ramos said, smiling. "Maybe they're right," he shrugged, "who knows? When are we leaving for Moktar, father?"

"I'm just a human suffering from a severe case of mistaken identity," Mac said.

"We'll leave after we eat. Kim, Mac, please join us in the dining room for some fresh deer stew." Gregor said.

An hour later the party of five was on their way out of town, headed for the centaur citadel of Moktar. Dante and Ramos slung their crossbows across their backs, and Gregor wielded his ornate wooden staff, the top of which had the skull of a small animal and ruby-red gems in the eye sockets. The humans carried their rifles, but Mac wore new clothes since his old ones were scraps. The group walked to the town center and stood before a golden statue of an ancient wolven warrior. A wolven woman stood before them.

"May the gods watch over you and protect you on your journey."

The wolven woman said. She bowed toward the party with her hands clasped like a pyramid.

"Thank you, Miranda. May they also protect and watch over this village until our safe return." Gregor said He bowed his head toward her as they passed.

Mac began to feel that familiar sinking, swimming nausea in his stomach and head again, the same as just before the last change. The wolven had been gracious enough to clothe him in leather with an elastic, stretchy material connecting the pieces. To him, they felt almost like magical clothes; they would not tear if and when he changed again. Mac felt the wolf breathe within him and saw its toothy maw when he closed his eyes. When they were beyond the village, Mac lurched forward as if he were about to vomit, and in less than thirty seconds he had changed back into the white wolven and stood looking confused at the surprised faces of his comrades.

"What?" He asked.

"Nothing, my friend. Your looks have improved a great deal in a short time." Ramos said.

"Wow. That is a neat trick, earthman!" Dante was stupefied. "Did you do that at will?"

Mac looked down at his hands and forearms, disturbed to see they were fur-covered, and his fingernails were now long black claws. He stumbled backward slamming his head into a branch he had walked under a moment ago.

"AAARGHHH!" He screamed.

"Mac, this situation may be permanent, so you might want to come to grips with it.." Gregor said. "I'm OK. I wish whatever this is would decide which way it wants to go. I mean, I want to learn to control it. This would scare the hell out of my kids if I just popped into wolf form out of nowhere." Mac said.

"Wolven." Ramos corrected. "Right, sorry," Mac said.

"There are sizable advantages for wolven. Pick up that rock over there." Ramos said.

"You mean the one about the size of my head?

No way, I can't lift that." Mac said.

"No, not the tiny rock. Pick up the one beside it." The other rock was a large boulder sunken deep into the ground.

"Are you kidding? Look at how deep it's buried. Besides, the last boulder I encountered was alive." Mac said and looked back at Ramos.

Ramos shook his head with the impatience of a frustrated teacher. "There are no such things as living boulders. There are enchanted boulders, however."

"How did they get that way?" Kim asked. "Before the end of the age of the golden sun,

there was an imbalance of power between the pyramids when our Tablet of Destinies was lost. The tablet is an object of enormous power, and it is said that whoever controls the tablet will rule the universe. During the war, the wolven and Minotaur were losing badly to Broad Axe, the reptilian king, who sought to take the tablet and rule many worlds. Still, Multok the Wise, chief of the Minotaur clan, went on a quest to finish the war by using the tablet against our enemies. Then he disappeared, along with the tablet. When the tablet was no longer in place to steady the power of the pyramids, instability ensued and caused many sleeping objects in this world to awaken in the form of magical imbalance. Foul creatures began to roam the land, giving rise to monsters like the centaurs and our enemy, Asura. We don't have time to waste, so if you do possess the power of the wolven, we need to see how much strength you gained from Gregor." Ramos said.

Mac looked at the boulder that, in his estimation, had to weigh more than a ton. With a mixture of doubt and excitement, he knelt, uprooting it from the ground, with the ease of a child lifting a whiffle ball, exposing a three-foot crater in the ground.

"Toss it at...that dead tree over there," Ramos said. He pointed toward a large tree about sixty feet from them that had long ago been struck by lightning. Mac hoisted the rock above his head and tossed it through the air with ease.

"Hey, what the..." The rock cried, and then it hit like a bomb, sending a shower of wood through the air. "Ow, my head!"

"Sorry," Mac said.

"It's alright." The rock said from a distance and went back to sleep.

"Nice throw!" Dante said. "You're gonna' do OK here."

"That was actually really easy," Mac said.

Ramos clapped him on the shoulder and nodded approval. Mac remained in wolven form until early evening when it was time to find a spot to camp for the night. He changed back to human form unexpectedly. Mac and Kim had the inflatable shelters from their backpacks, but the wolven needed no shelter. Dante disappeared for thirty minutes after the camp was set up and returned with a full-grown deer. To Mac and Kim, the animal looked like some cross between an ibex and a moose.

He walked into camp, put the animal carcass on a spit he'd crafted from a small green tree, and roasted it over a medium flame. The sun had set, and the camp firelight flickered against faces, half obscured by darkness, as each party member sat with a full belly.

Gregor filled a small metal cup with water and dropped a small green crystal into it. Smoke and fizz rose from the container, wafting up into the night. He looked over at Kim.

"Drink and pass," Gregor said. "What is it?" Kim asked.

"The vehicle for our journey," Gregor answered, and Ramos laughed.

"You're about to hear colors again, Kim," Ramos said.

The drink makes its way around the circle to Mac.

"Whew, that's stout." Mac winced and passed it back to Gregor.

Gregor produced a small green stone from a pocket in his robe and placed it in the fire. It rose from the flames a moment later and began to spin, throwing off light in every direction, displaying a visual projection of Gregor's story while he talked. They could all see a large rectangular star craft descending from the blue sky and smaller ships detaching from it, speeding away to the four points of the compass. The movie showed wolves, bulls, and other animals from this planet milling about, hunting prey, and carrying on the daily business of their lives.

"Millions of years ago travelers came from the stars. These were scientists sent to scour the universe for life and improve living conditions. They found it on Eritria in the form of numerous races of animals. These men of science evaluated our planet and inhabitants and decided that intervention was required to advance our society to the next level."

Gregor paused to make sure he had not confused Mac and Kim. In the movie, the little ships began to land, ramps descending, and little gray men with large heads and almond-shaped black eyes exiting.

"The creators sent the grey men, androids really, to genetically modify our DNA," Gregor said.

"How do you know about DNA? No offense, but scientists on our planet have only known about it for about a hundred years or so." Kim asked.

"We've known about DNA for about fifty-five thousand years. Our culture has detailed records of medical science dating back to our creation." Dante said.

"We've had at least four major cataclysmic events that wiped most of our records from the earth, and what wasn't taken by natural disaster, our people burned or destroyed in mad power grabs throughout history. We probably had the science a long time ago, but for some reason, our race seems to always slip back into dark ages." Mac said, shaking his head.

"The creators built those pyramids, which are still standing today. They could tap into the vibratory life of our world, transmitting communication to their home planet far from here. The pyramids were left behind when the scientists had completed their work, and later, we figured out how to use them for our own culture." Gregor's firestone displayed the grey men constructing the massive ziggurats with what may have been electro-gravitic machines. Solid granite blocks, weighing tons, floated through the air as if carried by invisible titans. In the next scene, tall humans garbed in silver skintight suits led rows of animals into the ziggurat structures through an opening at the top.

"Oh, they created *you* by genetic modification," Mac said. "We have similar tales on our planet. I have heard stories that giant sky gods called Anunnaki came from far away and modified a race of evolving humans thousands of years ago."

Mac looked back into the firestone images and saw that sometime after the animals had entered the ziggurats on four legs, they emerged walking upright. Minotaur, ibex, mole men, wolven, reptilians, and libmok's.

"What about the centaurs? I don't see any of them coming out of those temples." Mac asked.

"The centaurs are abominations created during the last great war with Broad Axe, father of Asura. A terrible space-time rift was opened during the final battle, causing many anomalies that unleashed unstable energies. The torsos of fairies were fused to the bodies of horses when the faerie cavalry passed through the cloud, creating the centaurs. We could have welcomed the new creatures into our society, had they been willing to assimilate. But the experience in the rift poisoned their minds, and since that time, the centaurs have been the enemy of the free people of Eritria. Broad Axe was pulled into the rift and his son, Asura, has been looking for him ever since by using the aid of demonic shades. Once Broad Axe was gone, the libmok's and other evil creatures from the bog lands receded, and we were left in peace, for a few hundred years anyway."

"So, they're planning a war with the wolven now?" Mac asked.

"That's what Rasp told us when he made it to Wasatch village. He snuck into Scowl castle and overheard a conversation between Ragnok, the centaur king, and Yawl, his lackey. The libmok's saw Rasp leaving and gave chase as he bolted back to the river, where they caught up to him, and that's when we came along to his aid." Dante said. "And now that they have the Shadow Blade and our cosmic portal, there is no telling what mischief they may conjure."

"They could raise the army of Ardeuceus to fight alongside them and the libmoks," Ramos said.

"But, for the cosmic portal, they still need this." Mac held up the controller.

"Double Head feels you humans are too dangerous to be left alive," Gregor said.

"What do you think?" Mac asked.

"I believe much remains to be seen. We have been told of your coming for hundreds of years, but not exactly to what end. We're also being tracked by Double Head, so be on your guard." Gregor replied.

Clouds had been gathering in the dark sky above, and when they cleared, the twin moons of Eritria appeared. They had a red tint to them, like the eyes of a monster in the sky. Ramos doubled over in pain, wincing in silence beside Mac.

"The blood moons are upon me, father," Ramos said. His teeth were clenched together. "I didn't think it would come so soon."

"I knew the time would be close," Gregor said. "I saw this in my sleep the other night."

"What are the blood moons?" Kim asked. "Ramos is about to experience the change.

He'll have to go to the Cave of Tholuman and complete the trial of undeath. As the first-born son of the village chief, when he was twelve years old, a traveling witch doctor came to our village, and Ramos was given a choice either to become a chief or to walk the path of the necromancer. The blood moons only appear once every three years, and now, since Ramos is of age, he must complete his quest to become a necromancer. It's an honor given to the chosen, for few are, and few survive the challenge. Asura went on the same journey and fell to madness in that cave." Gregor said.

"It is said great evil lives inside the mountain," Ramos said. He was sitting up now, and the pain seemed to have passed. "I'll have to leave you all in the morning, once we get to the plains." "Let me get this straight. We're headed to Moktar, the stronghold for your mortal enemy, and Ramos is leaving us to go finish a quest to raise the undead?" Mac asked.

"Yes of course," Gregor said. He was nodding to his sons.

"Use your new ability to strike down your enemies, brother," Dante said.

Mac walked to the edge of their campsite, peering into the blackness beyond, feeling the eyes of million-night creatures on him as he stood on the doorstep of the deep, dark wilderness. As Mac stood at the edge of their firelight, the ground began to give way under his feet. Pebbles and dirt slid into a growing crevasse as Mac looked down, his eyes wide and mouth frozen in an O of surprise as his legs collapsed and he fell to the ground. He spent the next few seconds desperately grappling the ground and sliding downward. Dante turned just in time to see a tentacle fly up from beneath the Colonel's body and wrap around his waist.

"Trapdoor terapod! Ramos. We've got trouble!!" Dante screamed.

Mac understood immediately and felt the fire once more, only this time it was like a dull throb; his body began to lengthen, his strength grew, and his hands turned into claws as his maw snarled. He grabbed the tentacle with both paws and snapped it in two. The remaining tentacle slithered back into the ground as Mac forward rolled up and out of the pit. He stood on dry ground a moment later, looking down into the funnel while slowly backing away.

"Get ready, brother!" Dante said to Ramos. "This is going to be fun, remember the last time we fought one of..." Ramos said. Before he could finish, a thirty-foot-tall spider crab exploded out of the small hole into which it had previously been dragging Mac.

The trap door terapod loomed over them on spindly legs, a horror from Mac's spider-filled nightmares as a child. And now, standing in front of him was the biggest spider he had ever seen. It had a hard back shell and pincers on each side of a vertical mouth filled with sharp needle teeth. The sides of its body were writhing with tangles of thick tentacles, extending toward Mac in a hypnotic snake-like rhythm. Mac stood staring, dumbfounded at the living nightmare as Dante and Ramos dashed past him, leaping through the air with supernatural speed. Dante landed on the tetrapod's back, slashing at defending tentacles, while Ramos struck two legs.

"Mac, we could use your help, if you're done staring," Dante said.

"This is going to be fun; last time, you got to kill it. I've got dibs on this one, and Mac, avoid the mouth; they have a nasty bite! Ramos yelled. Kim fired at the monster with her plasma rifle her boss snapped out of it and grabbed a pincher, swiping for his head. He held on with both arms as it lifted him in the air, swinging him toward the rows of its teeth, dripping with a foul-smelling liquid. Dante stabbed down with his claws into the monster's back, tearing through the hard shell, while his brother removed two more legs. The tentacles on Ramos's side swept under his feet, caught him off balance, and wrapped around his ankle.

He was tossed through the air, slamming into a tree. As he recovered, it caught him again and dragged him across the ground until the monster raised him high above its gaping mouth. Before he could be tossed inside, Mac jerked his body with full force and snapped the claw off, sending him hurling to the ground. The terapod let out a hiss as a shot from Kim's rifle blasted half a row of acid-covered teeth from the creature's mouth. Dante punched down repeatedly, smashing the hard shell of the terapod, and reaching inside its back.

It tried to buck him off, but his determination would not be undone. While he was reaching inside the beast, Ramos ran back and dived at the terapod's exposed underbelly. Ramos smashed into it as if he were tearing through tissue paper and entered the monster's body with a sickening slurping sound. The terapod howled but was not down yet. Kim fired again, destroying the other pincher as Mac tore off three more tentacles and ripped off the terapod's eye stalks.

"These things are hard to kill!" Mac screamed. "They are indeed, and their holes are difficult to spot until you're right up on them," Gregor said. He was standing now, holding his staff. The jeweled eyes were glowing red in the darkness.

Dante reached down inside the creature and grabbed hold of something while the terapod dropped to the ground. A moment later Ramos emerged from the terapod's back, holding Dante's hand and covered from head to toe in goo.

"I want to take a month-long bath. Ugh, this is nasty." Ramos said.

He spat white goo onto the ground.

"Argh, you stink!" Dante said. He pulled Ramos the rest of the way out, and they jumped to the forest floor from the back of the thirty-foot- tall spider carcass.

"You try crawling through the intestines of a terapod and see how you smell, huh?" Ramos said.

They stared at one another for a moment until a brilliant red light emanated from Gregor's staff, engulfing the tetrapod's carcass in yellow and red flames, charring it to cinders in minutes. Mac thought it smelled like somebody's cat was on fire and turned his head in disgust.

"If that's the only one of these we see on this adventure we can consider ourselves fortunate," Gregor said.

"I'm going to the river to clean this mess off of me," Ramos said.

As he walked off into the darkness, Dante stood with Gregor watching his brother go.

"I regret that Yawl took the Shadow Blade from me, father. I only hope to right things before..."

At that moment, a puff of smoke wisps through the air as Double Head materialized before them and pinned Dante to a tree by his neck.

"Yawl did what? You might have just brought about world war with your foolishness, Dante!" Double Head growled.

Gregor shot a force blast from his staff, knocking Double Head to the ground.

"We are fixing the problem, Double Head!" Gregor shouted.

Double Head stood, brushing himself off. "Where's the blade now? You don't know, do you?"

Gregor closed his eyes and fell into a meditative state. After a few moments, he opened them, casting his gaze to the ground.

"Lonas is walking across the desert; the Shadow Blade is in his belt. I also saw a high- walled castle and a statue of the lion god Artytrix, but he is still a day away." Gregor said.

"I thought as much." Double Head barked and pointed the finger of accusation at Dante.

"Lonas is going to the castle of Gaelen the Bloodthirsty, the final stronghold of the faerie kingdom." He finished.

Ramos walks back into the light, but clean. "And if he makes it there, he will raise the army of King Ardeuceus," Ramos said.

Dante stood defiantly against the large Chief. "I don't know how I obtained the blade!"

"Your lack of mental acuity allowed the spirits within the blade to beguile you into releasing it from the artifact vault. Let's go!" Double Head commanded.

Dante looks to Gregor in disbelief.

"Double Head is right, Dante. If Lonas succeeds, there will be chaos." Gregor said.

"Fine, let's get this over with," Dante said. As Dante and Double Head walked out of the camp, Double Head fixed the humans with disdain.

"While we're away, Gregor, you might reconsider keeping these pets of yours alive. Sentimentality and folklore never obscure my visions; the THEY are trouble."

Double Head and Dante walked into the night, leaving Mac, Kim, and Ramos behind. Mac watched Double Head with steely eyes, tickled the trigger of his rifle, and almost brought it up to shoulder height when Kim whispered next to him.

"Don't prove them right, sir."

"I'm leaving as well, father. The Cave of Tholuman is a day's run, and I feel the time is growing short."

Gregor and Ramos embraced tightly. Then Gregor retrieved a locket from his pocket and placed it around Ramos's neck.

"Mother's locket," Ramos said.

"Open it, and the magic within will carry you short distances from your enemies," Gregor said. "I'll return in one day, if at all. Don't wait too long." Ramos said. He smiled at Mac and Kim.

"Good luck," and vanished into the night.

Mac lay on his back, staring at the stars for the rest of the night in wolven form, wondering if things would ever be the same again and half hoping they never would.

CHAPTER 10

RAGNOK, KING OF THE CENTAURS, stood frowning as he surveyed his land from the top of Scowl Castle in the heart of Moktar.

"Well?" Ragnok said.

He was speaking to three shades, staring into a bubbling cauldron. They were ethereal creatures, formless and purely evil beings from the fifth dimension, which provided counsel to the hotheaded centaur king. They had been watching the cauldron since the human woman arrived at Scowl Castle. It bubbled and churned a green liquid that emitted a putrid scent, like rotten eggs boiled in sulfur.

"These humans very well may be the ones you have been waiting for all this time, Ragnok." One whispered.

"They have many powerful weapons at their command." One shade whispered.

"Excellent, Asura will be pleased," Ragnok said.

Yawl entered the room.

"What do you want?" Ragnok asked.

"My lord, the female refuses to tell us anything. Would you like me to tear her arms off?" Yawl asked.

Ragnok thought about it momentarily, rubbing his chin with his right hand.

"No, but we could set her free with the device and make sure she gets back to her people," Ragnok said.

"I can make sure the humans open that portal again and then steal it from them."

Ragnok admired the Shadow Blade. "I can't wait to plunge this weapon into Gregor's heart after we awaken the army of Ardeuceus. And then, I'll kill his sons. Go, unlock her cell." "Yes sir, as you wish," Yawl said.

Stephanie had been sitting with her back against the cold wall of a dank dungeon cell, frightened, alone, and chilled to her bones. a lit torch on the wall outside her cell was the only light. She heard moans and groans from nearby cells where those driven mad by captivity spouted obscenities into the gloom. The insanity of their calls was maddening, and her spirit sank with each passing hour.

Pushed and prodded to her cell by centaur guards, beaten and bruised along the way, she had seen a number of medieval torture devices. Stretching racks held the wire-thin corpses of the emaciated dead and dying. Other victims, pathetic imprisoned creatures dangled from the walls like miserable marionettes. One of the people strapped to the rack was a half-wolven, half-lizard man who shouted that the centaurs would never subjugate him.

A three-foot-tall man resembling a mole was ushered into an iron maiden, sobbing as he entered the spike-filled chamber. Stephanie could hear him pleading for his life, crying, and begging them to let him go until the door slammed shut. Silence and a trickle of blood ran from beneath the door into a drain. Three porcupine men were crucified to a board by their hands and feet, and a few of the centaur guards were using them as target practice with their bows and arrows. One of the guards had a large, deadly crossbow in his hands and had already put two bolts through one porcupine man's knees.

This was all Stephanie could see as the guard, using a prod to move her along, marched her down one filthy hallway after another toward the cold cell where she currently sat, wishing she were anywhere else. Her treatment had been appalling, and she could not figure out what she had done to deserve such a fate. She paced the cell and found it was no bigger than seven feet by seven feet, and the ceiling was only two inches above her head.

If she stood on the balls of her feet, she would bang her head on the rock roof of her cell. Beyond the physical confines and the darkness, her cell was rife with the odor of stale urine. She was dwelling on her misery when she heard a scratching, clinking sound on the other side of her cell door.

"Food! Wretch! Eat!" A male voice yelled.

The door swung open, and a plate with something wriggling on it was shoved through her cell door. She could see it was still alive in the half-light and seemed to be a cross between a cockroach and a caterpillar. Her gag reflex took hold, and she felt warm, stinging bile rise in the back of her throat. She never saw the delivery man, and her door slammed shut a moment later. Stephanie waited to hear the lock turn and seal her in, but it never did. Her mind began to race, sure that at any moment, the man would remember his folly and come back to lock her in again, but he never did.

Suddenly, she was terrified that he would never return and that she had what might only be a brief window to escape. Millions of butterflies fluttered in her stomach. The roach- caterpillar thing was squealing now, emitting an eerie sound that made Stephanie want to escape that much more in the darkness and loneliness of her cell. The critter wriggled out of its plate and crawled half onto the floor as she curiously watched its black form move.

"You and I both, pal. I'm getting out of here." She spoke.

Stephanie tried the door, expecting an electric shock or that the handle would turn into a venomous snake. Visions of a horde of centaurs waiting to pounce on the other side of the door played in her mind, but she could hear nothing. She pressed lightly, and the black iron door swung open on rusty hinges, the hanging torch bathing her face with grim, flickering light from the hallway. Screams of agony, moans from the condemned, and an odor of rotten meat permeated the air she breathed as Stephanie tried to remember from which direction she had come. The hallways stretched into darkness in either direction, disorienting her even more. Returning to the little bug in her cell, which had already crawled halfway to where she had been sitting, she shuddered and closed the cell door with the quietness of a church mouse.

Stephanie decided to go right and passed by one cell after another of pathetic, condemned souls, staring through small—head-sized— barred portals out at her. Life or death, *your* life or death, get out of here and fast, she thought. One or two cellmates spat in her direction, a few grunted and spoke in a language she had never heard, and she was almost sure they were cussing at her.

"I haven't gotten out yet." She whispered under her breath.

The corridor ended, and around a corner, she was confronted with the most horrific.

Frankenstein-like laboratory she had ever seen. Her father would watch slasher films with her as a child, the kind of grindhouse films that were specifically designed to turn the stomachs of squeamish viewers and torture their senses. She had seen a movie once where a madman in a mask made from human skin chased smart- mouthed twenty-somethings around an old two- story western manor, seeing them in two with a chainsaw. The lunatic parade went on until all of their corpses were strung up and treated like sides of beef for a cannibalistic family.

The movie haunted her dreams for months, and she never watched it again. The chainsaw massacre paled compared to what she witnessed in this dungeon, however. Slabs of meat were piled on wooden tables with butcher knives sticking out of them in pools of thick, dark blood as flies buzzed around the rotting matter with hungry eyes and bellies. Bodies that had been torn in half, like tissue paper, dangled from meat hooks bolted to the ceiling.

Torches on the walls and support posts illuminated the grizzly scene, but what surprised her most was the creature she saw in front of her, chained to a far wall. The thing looked at her wearily with the head and neck of a Minotaur stitched to the shoulders of a centaur-like deranged jigsaw puzzle.

The creature had been sleeping a moment earlier until it heard her enter the lab and its eyes popped open with a start.

"Don't, *cough, cough*, leave me here." The beast croaked. She began to feel ashamed of her fear and sorry for the abomination. All four legs had been chained to the wall, giving it no room to move.

"Kill me. You must kill me. Please, set me free." The abomination said and nodded to a crossbow sitting on a table next to several crossbow bolts.

Stephanie walked over and picked up the crossbow, knocked a bolt, and turned back toward the abomination.

As if it sensed her hesitation. "I was dead the moment Ragnok did this to me. Do it before they come back."

The monster was pathetic and alone, so she lifted the crossbow and took aim.

"The crossbow. Use it."

Stephanie squinted her eyes and squeezed the trigger. The bolt entered the pathetic creature's head, and as it did, the body went limp, hanging from its chains like a marionette, and it let out a final, hollow exhale.

"I'm sorry." She said and dropped the crossbow to the floor.

Stephanie ran down the hall and through another passage where she overheard two guards, a man and a woman talking casually from an adjacent room. She stopped in her tracks, flattening against the wall.

"Yawl said the invasion would begin after the blood moons rose, but that was days ago, and I haven't heard another word about it." The man said.

"That was before the strange craft arrived, and that box came out of it." The woman asked. "Strange object, that box. You know what it does?" The man asked.

"No, Yawl wouldn't say, even after he met with Ragnok. But I think the shades know what it is."

"What about the human woman? You know what they're going to do with her?" The man said.

"What about the human woman? You know what they're going to do with her?" She asked. Stephanie heard them moving on and waited with bated breath until the coast was clear. She peered around the corner but saw nobody was there and darted past the door. She came across two more corridors and found a staircase leading up. Beside the stairs was another room with a large wooden plank door half-open.

Stephanie walked up to the door and peered into the room. She was surprised to find the cosmic portal sitting on a table in the center of the room. With quiet footsteps, she walked over to the table, picked up the cosmic portal with both hands, and ran out the door.

Stephanie ran up a staircase to an upper-level floor that led to a courtyard outside. Again, nobody was around, but she could see some centaur guards about a hundred yards away with their backs turned away from her. Stephanie took her prize and ran for the door, ducking low behind a hedgerow. There was a small hole in the castle wall that was just large enough for her to crawl through with the cosmic portal.

"OK, let's do it!" She whispered to herself.

Ten minutes later, she was free of the castle walls and running across an open field toward a grove of twisted, misshapen trees on the border of a deep forest. She knew she'd find some cover once she passed the tree line.

Yawl stood next to Ragnok as they watched her run into the Bog Lands, the bleak and ancient forest many had entered, with few to return.

"Make sure she gets through the bog lands, but don't let her see you," Ragnok said.

Yawl bowed his head and walked out of the room.

"Lonas!" Ragnok yelled.

Lonas entered the room and bowed. "Yes, sir."

Ragnok turned toward him with the hilt of the Shadow Blade facing him.

"Take the Shadow Blade to the statue of Artytrix and wake our sleeping cousins, the faeries of King Ardeuceus."

"As you wish," Lonas said. He bowed and left.

Ragnok turned to his mirror, and the reflective surface began to shimmer until the image of a large lizard man in a black robe appeared before Ragnok.

"Asura, we are almost ready for war. Yawl will find the mechanism that activates the cosmic portal, and Lonas will wake the sleeping faeries, and then we can attack."

"Good, very good." Asura hissed. "

Behind Asura, in the half-light, Ragnok could see the silhouette of an undead warrior shambling toward his master. The ghoul had once been a reptilian soldier years ago but now survived off the flesh of the living creatures Asura tossed at it. A rat in his hand squirmed to break free of the dark lord's grip.

"My army of the undead allied with your centaurs, faeries, and the libmok's will wash over this land and bathe it in wolven and Minotaur blood," Asura said, smiling wickedly. "You've done well Ragnok, and soon it will be your time to rule Eritria."

The image of Asura faded, leaving Ragnok alone in his chambers. He walked over to the window overlooking his fields and watched the earth woman running with the rectangular, metallic cosmic portal held in her arms. Ragnok grinned with malevolence as Stephanie disappeared into the bog lands.

CHAPTER 11

DANTE AND DOUBLE HEAD HIKED through the night to the edge of the plains, southwest of the Bog Lands, and entered the desert. Tall buttes and mesas greet them as the lush green plains fade into the distance, replaced by a harsh, unforgiving landscape. Far from them, shimmering like a mirage, are the high onyx walls of Gaelen the Bloodthirsty's castle. Built into the side of a cliff, the walls jutted into the morning sky like a diseased tooth. Their high mirror polish gleams in the new day sun.

Hoofprints were visible in the sand, blowing away with the wind. Dante knelt, feeling the print, and then looked at Double Head.

"Lonas was here," Dante said. The two began to run.

Lonas galloped across the desert at a slow pace; carrying a two-handed war hammer on his right, with a sword sheathed at his side on the left. The Shadow Blade fit neatly into his belt, and he smiled as the statue of Artytrix formed in his vision across the expanse of bleak desert. Gaelen the Bloodthirsty, long ago having abandoned the centaurs to their fate, whatever that may be, would be no help to him, but Ardeuceus may not only honor their old alliance but happily join in the fight for Eritria for their release from obscurity inside the world of the blade.

Closer now, he could see the fifty-foot-tall basalt monument glimmering with soft azure light from the blue crystals peppering his surface. As Lonas closed the distance, the crystals reacted to the blade and began to glow radiantly. A wicked grin spread across his face. It would not be long now. From behind him, he could hear the beating feet of two interlopers, and when he turned, he saw Dante and Double Head.

Dante and Double Head raced across the desert and finally found Lonas fifty yards from the statue, the basalt glowing with supernatural brilliance. Dante felt a pang of fear and dread. When he looked over at Double Head, the more experienced Chief wore a mask of utter stoicism. Lonas did not turn to fight but began to race toward the statue.

Dante picked up his pace and dived into Lonas's rear legs, slashing with lightning reflexes, and severing muscles in the centaur's left hind quarter. Lonas swung around with his war hammer and caught Double Head in the left shoulder as he was leaping through the air.

Double Head reels, and hits the ground, regaining his feet in a matter of seconds.

Lonas stopped running and turned on Dante as Double Head snuck up from behind and placed the centaur in a headlock. Lonas was twenty feet from the statue, and mist began to roll along the ground, low and ethereal. Dante stood up, and punched Lonas in the jaw, using the claws of his other hand to impale their foe's abdomen. Lonas choked, his face contorting from the pain, and dropped to the ground.

Double Head took the dagger from Lonas's belt as Dante glared wickedly at him. Dante, without warning, punched Double Head in the face and snatched the blade out of the air as Double Head dropped it. Whispers float on the breeze as the mist turns into a fog, illuminated by the ever-growing light beaming from Artytrix.

"If any part of that dagger touches the statue we will have an entire risen army on our hands, Dante!" Double Head yelled.

Double Head picked up the war hammer and kicked Dante in the back. Dante let out a grunt and sprawled to the ground, as the dagger skidded across the hard ground. Double Head picked up the blade, placed it on a flat rock, and with one mighty swing, he brought the hammer down, smashing the Shadow Blade into several pieces. A geyser of blue-green light erupts from the blade straight into the sky, burning away the fog and parting the clouds. Enormous thunderclap booms as the last of the souls trapped with that blade fade into the blue atmosphere.

Double Head turns the war hammer on Dante.

"Is your head clear, Dante?!"

Dante waves a passive hand in the air wearily as he sits up. "I'm fine, thank you."

Double Head helps him up, and the two sit on an outcropping of rocks. Double Head placed a hand on Dante's shoulder.

"Mesmerized, by a dagger. Fantastic." Dante shook his head.

"Don't beat yourself up, Dante. When your father and I were younger, I fell in love with Gilda the Enchantress, and she almost turned me into a toad. Ha! Ha! Gregor..."

Double head stopped short as a sword passed through his abdomen from behind. Lonas had managed to pull himself across the desert floor and in one last foul deed, he mortally wounded the wolven Chief, and then Lonas died where he lay. Double Head dropped to his knees reaching behind him to pull the sword out, his face a mask of pained determination.

Dante picked up the war hammer and smashed Lonas's head with it in several enraged blows, leaving the deceased centaur unrecognizable. Dante walked over to Double Head, dropped the hammer, and knelt down as the misunderstood Chief fell to his side. Double Head was struggling to breathe.

"Beware of the humans, young chieftain. Their untethered reign means death to us all."

Before Dante could say another word, Double Head exhaled his final breath and lay still, staring up at the sky as he died. Dante bowed his head, shook it in disbelief, and stood. As he walked away, the statue of Artytrix began to crumble.

One day later, Mac, Kim, and Gregor were living aboard the *Poseidon*, waiting for Dante, Double Head, and Ramos to return as the sun rose on another sun-filled. Dante returned the previous afternoon with the tragic news regarding Double Head's demise, and that night Gregor held a ceremony to allow the spirit of his old friend to pass to the next world in peace. Mac woke to a beam of sun shining in his face and stood up to stretch when he saw a woman running across the plains holding a familiar object in her arms. Mac saw her first and grabbed his binoculars.

"It's Stephanie! She's got the cosmic portal with her!" Mac yelled.

"Oh, thank God!" Kim said, whispering, " This nightmare is almost over."

"She's got company!" Mac said. He could see she was being followed by libmok's and running just in front of them. The cosmic portal was clutched in her arms as she sprinted toward the spacecraft, and Mac could see that the libmok's were gaining. He turned wolven in a matter of moments and darted across the prairie.

"Mac, wait!" Dante said.

Mac closed the distance between him and Stephanie and saw the look of terror and confusion on her face as he got nearby. He could smell her intoxicating fear.

"Captain Brandt, nice to see you alive!" "Mac?" She asked.

Without time to explain, he darted past her,

knocking the lead libmok off its feet and tearing the creature's throat out with his sharp claws. Two more of them remained and faced off against him with their quills raised, each grabbing a poisoned sword from their backs for defense.

"Not this time, boys!" Mac said.

He rolled forward and slashed up with one powerful strike into the next one's stomach, disemboweling the surprised libmok. It took two steps back and fell over in a heap. Dante grabbed a quill off the first dead libmok and stabbed the last one through his chest. It uttered a squeak in retaliation and dropped to the ground as dead as his brothers. Mac could sense presence hiding at the edge of the Bog Lands three hundred yards away. He stopped and turned his sensitive nose to the breeze.

"Mac, is that really you?" Stephanie asked. "There have been some...changes. How are you? How did you get away from the centaurs?" Mac asked. Gregor walked out to greet them as they neared The Poseidon.

"They let her go." He said, his nose in the air, sniffing. "Yawl followed you. His foul stench is on the breeze, and I have a feeling we'll be seeing them soon enough."

"Yawl is watching us," Dante said. His eyes scanned the trees but discovered nothing.

Mac turned toward Stephanie and changed back to his human form again; he was gaining more control over his ability to do so each time. "My God, that's amazing. If we ever do get a real laboratory built here, I need to study your condition." Stephanie marveled.

"Maybe I'm the beginning of a whole new race of men." Mac winked at her.

"Let's get back to the ship and close it up for the night. There's been enough drama for one day." Mac said. Gregor walked beside Stephanie, the cosmic portal still in her arms.

"I've never asked how this device works. Do you know?" Gregor asked. Mac was a few feet behind him and heard Gregor's question.

"You have to think about where you want to go, and then press the button on this controller. Easy." Mac said.

Dante dragged the carcass of a libmok back to the ship with them. Hearing the grass rustle, Mac turned to see what he was doing.

"Wolven's gotta' eat, and these are damned fine in a pinch," Dante said, grinning.

They built a small fire to roast the libmok. As the sun set on another day, they all entered the *Poseidon* for a night of safety and good sleep. Mac closed his weary eyes, and for the first time in a year, he did not dream. A snow-capped mountain loomed over Ramos as he approached the Cave of Tholuman. A dark mouth yawned like an ancient giant and opened into an underground world of unknown perils and mystery. Ramos strode across the plains where his forefathers battled Broad Axe, Ragnok, the reptilian army, the faeries of Ardeuceus, the centaurs, and an army of the undead, hundreds of years before. He saw faint impressions of his fallen ancestor's spirits, engaged in spectral reenactment, and heard their swords clanging together as a long-ago war raged on in another dimension. Ramos pressed on, ignoring them. The odor of death touched his nostrils as Ramos neared the Cave of Tholuman. Ramos steeled his nerves, let go of unslung his crossbow,

placed it on the ground, and walked into the cave.

Upon entering, the daylight receded, and his way out became blocked by a black wall of impenetrable magic. He was engulfed in darkness as if a veil had been drawn and there he stood, alone. Purple gems illuminated a pathway through the darkness, showing him the way into the cave. Ramos felt the temperature drop so low that he could see his breath chuffing out in little white clouds.

As he stood watching the little gems pop to life, one after another, disappearing around a bend, Ramos began to feel a tremor in the floor beneath his feet, and a surge of nausea swept over him.

He stooped, hands on knees, riding the wave of pain in his stomach when a mind-bending cramp seized him. Ramos doubled over with nausea, howled in agony, and blew out his last breath as his soul rose from his body. He stood emotionless over his still-breathing body, and then he turned and glided forward through the ether.

After following the spiral path downward for some time, a white light appeared before him, shimmering in the dark and reflecting off the stone walls. When he came around another bend, he saw a female humanoid that resembled, in great detail, the humans from earth. She was bathed in white light. Her complexion was fair; her long blond hair hung down around her face, and she wore a loose- fitting white peasant shirt with white pants. The ethereal angel stopped and stared at Ramos for a moment before speaking.

"Welcome Ramos, I am Kahli, the spirit of the Cave of Tholuman. Have you come seeking the trial Quezal?" She spoke. Her voice was soft and reverberated as it echoed through the cavern.

"I have," Ramos replied.

"Ramos of the Blood Paw, you will gaze into the Oracle and she into you. If you survive the test, you will become a warlock." Kahli said. He followed her down until the tunnel opened up to a large brightly lit cavern. A temple carved from the cavern walls loomed above them. Its height was impressive, but the ornate carvings of deer, fox, owl, and bulls were awe inspiring. Their lifelike statues decorated the balconies like omniscient guardians, and their shadows swayed as if they were watching Ramos' every move.

"All you see before you were carved from a single rock face hundreds of thousands of years ago by a race of people long extinct," Kahli said.

She pointed to a large set of double doors that had begun opening. Ramos looks around with suspicion as he realizes that the entire floor is covered in a blanket of bones.

"How many more of you are hiding down here?" Ramos asked.

Ramos saw the form of a man as he floated a few feet above the floor. His hands beckoned Ramos forth. A purple orb rested on a pedestal behind the ghostly form.

"Ravi will show you the way forward," Kahli said.

Ramos drifted forward, toward a man in a black robe with gold trim threaded on the sleeves and around the neckline. A hypnotic melody began to play in Ramos' conscious mind, luring him into a slow loss of memory and identity. The temple was closer, larger, and something unseen beckoned to him as he drifted toward the purple orb and his destiny.

Ramos was between dimensions then, a galactic traveler faded beyond the confines of the cavern. Reality began to slide away until Ramos was someplace peaceful where flowers and wolven women draped over couches smiling as he walked by, calling to him.

Ravi grinned with a mouth full of fangs and eyes of a snake, with a hypnotic yellow glow that fumed and pulsed. Ramos turned around and saw that Kahli was standing behind him,

and her appearance was much the same, but her eyes were no longer shining, and they had sunken into her skull.

"Now! Ravi, grab him!" Kahli screamed.

Ramos held his mother's locket and was behind Ravi in an instant as the ghoul sprang forth to devour his soul. Ramos raced inside the double doors before they could grab him and held the orb with both hands. The energy within the purple ball pulsed outward, seizing his spectral arm while rivulets of purple light consumed him, burning his soul with the intensity of its flame.

"No! Ravi, grab him! We have to stop him before he..." Kahli screamed.

"So much power! Ramos moaned, as his soul convulsed in the purple, spectral light.

He lifted the orb from the pedestal, his hands frozen around it as the spirit within invaded his mind. Ramos was transported to a beach, watching from above as a massive tidal wave slammed into the shore. Skyscrapers are washed away like twigs, floating away in an angry ocean. A moment later, he and Dante stand together, back-to-back, against a horde of demons in a desert landscape unlike any he had ever seen.

"Go now, necromancer, warlock, and summoner of lost souls." A female voice within the orb whispered.

Ramos howled as his eyes turned a shade of deep lavender, and in that moment, he could hear the dead in the cavern speaking to him, whispering his name. Ramos materialized before the specter's, his body becoming whole once more glaring at his attempted murderers with enraged, glowing purple eyes, enraged. Purple orbs emanated from his hands, spinning, and floating like tiny planets above his outstretched paws. The cursed lovers stopped and looked at him with fear in their eyes.

"Any last words?" Ramos said. He wasn't sure if he had the ability to do such a thing, but they seemed fearful of him now, so he was going with it.

"Please don't do this; you now have the power to release us!" Ravi said.

"For your mercy, we will tell you where to find an artifact so powerful that you can defend against the darkest magic!" Khali pleaded.

"Yes! The Robe of Dragaz! It is imbued with the power to resist dark magic, collect the energy, and direct it back to the summoner." Ravi said.

"Where is it?" Ramos asked.

"It is below this temple, but you will have to speak with Inga the dragon and answer her riddle to obtain it," Kahli said.

"This will be worth your time because it is said the robe contains the power of ten armies."

The purple orbs hovering above his hands turn pink, and he cast them toward the spirits.

"Farewell, Ramos," Ravi said.

The two smile at Ramos and vanish into thin air. Ramos turns and spots a stairwell leading down into the cavern.

"This had better be worth it."

He began walking down sidestepping piles of skulls scattered along the corridor, the stale odor of death permeating the air. After a matter of moments, he came to a dead end. Before him in the path was a stone wall with seven ornate runes carved into the surface. As he approached a jade green glow emanated from them.

"It's a puzzle," Ramos said.

He studied it closer and realized there was a method to the shapes. They symbolized the seven teachings of the wolven people, common knowledge about how all people were to treat one another and live in peaceful coexistence with nature and other creatures. They were out of order, but he remembered the story that Gregor would tell Dante and him when they were children.

As the story replayed in his mind, Ramos began to picture the shapes in order. The deer symbolized the need to respect nature as they had once been wiped out by over-hunting but eventually returned strong. When the creator was about to destroy the world because his creatures could not stop fighting each other, he sent an ibis to fly around the world and see if any love still existed. When the ibis flew back, he reported that the wolven race still had a love for one another and the animals. The bilichuck, a creature resembling a beaver, was master of water and wood, symbolizing wisdom. The wolven ancestors had gained all their knowledge of medicines by watching the bilichuck.

Honesty was represented by the sprites, for they were given the responsibility of watching over all life on Eritria, and their honesty encourages all people to be honest with each other. Next was courage, represented by the Minotaur for their power and fearlessness to do the right thing and take care of their families and one another. The star shining light upon Eritria represented truth because the sun, like the creator, is true and no one in the infinite dimensions of space-time could change the sun. Things that are true never change. The wolven teach their young humility, to think things through and to always be cautious. Then an elderly wolven man, because the wolven people are never alone; they help one another. Wolven teach their young that they must look back on their lives and learn from it.

Ramos began to touch each symbol in the order of his father's tale, and as he did, they lit up until all seven were alive with color and the wall vanished before his eyes. Beyond the wall was a short corridor that opened to a larger cavern that extended far into the blackness. Inside the cavern, he could hear a large creature snoring in the darkness. Ramos willed a purple orb into existence that lit the path before him, and as he walked forward, it moved alongside him like a torch. The air was dank and cold like a crypt, but he feared nothing in this place where he knew the dragon would give him what he came for. As he moved into the cavern, claws scraped the hard stone floor, and he could see two golden eyes staring back at him. Ramos stood still.

"I know why you're here warlock. You should turn around and go home while you still can." Boomed a female voice.

A spark in the darkness ignited a large torch mounted on the wall and then another until the lights on the wall illuminated the entire cavern. Ramos could see that he was but a speck compared to the enormous green dragon before him. She was the biggest creature he had ever seen, and her size and beauty dumbfounded Ramos. But he still resisted feelings of intimidation.

"I'll have your riddle now, great dragon." "Failure means banishment of your soul to the shadow realm. There you will live out the rest of eternity in torment and sorrow." Inga said.

"I'll have your riddle now, if you would, please."

"Very well, you have two opportunities to answer. What begins the day on four legs, then two legs, then three?" Inga said.

Inga was seven stories tall, with luminescent green scales that shimmered in the light as if she were made of emeralds. She dipped her head, coming face to face with him, but he did not move. A distorted image of himself mirrored back at Ramos from her golden eyes, and for the first time since his change, Ramos saw the purple fire in his own eyes through the reflection.

"Give up?" Inga asked.

"A wolven man or woman. We walk on four legs as puppies, then on two legs as adults, and then on two legs with a cane when we grow old." Ramos said.

The dragon reared back for a moment as if stunned by his answer. Ramos began to feel as if he had made a horrible mistake, but then she lowered her head to three feet in front of him. Her white fangs popped through her lips as she sneered.

"That's right!" She spoke. Inga was grinning with pleasure. "This robe is nothing to take for granted, Ramos. The power imbued within the fabric can twist your soul." "I'll be careful," Ramos said.

"We shall see," Inga replied.

Inga whispered an incantation, and a dark portal opened. Through it, Ramos could see the void of space and the shape of something approaching him from the other side. The robe drifted through the portal and into his arms as he reached out and caught it on the way through. The Robe of Dragaz was maroon, with beautiful runic patterns sewn in with gold thread into the soft terrycloth-like fabric. He wasted no time putting the robe on while the portal shrunk to a speck and disappeared. As he put his arms through the sleeves, his energy level spiked like a volcano erupting within him, and he felt an exhilaration that seemed impossible to contain.

"The robe will amplify your positive or negative energy, Ramos. Take heed of my warning, and do not allow the negative energies to drag you into their web." Inga said.

"Thank you for your wise words, farewell, Inga," Ramos said. He donned the hood, and as he did, his glowing purple eyes were all that were visible.

"Farewell, warlock," Inga said.

Ramos began to walk back to where Dante and the people from Earth were camping. A day later he was approaching the spacecraft as the first rays of sunlight struck the reflective metallic surface. Dante emerged from the craft and walked over to his brother engaging him in a warm embrace.

"I thought I detected a foul odor in the air but didn't think you would be the source of it!" Dante said.

"It's good to see you again as well, little brother. Where is Double Head." Ramos said.

"Lonas killed him, but not before he destroyed the Shadow Blade," Dante replied. Ramos hung his head low.

"That's sad news. He was a good Chief." Ramos said.

"I misjudged him almost to the end," Dante said.

Ramos stood back from his brother.

"Dante, I've experienced many troubling visions since leaving the Cave of Tholuman. On the way back I saw war with the centaurs." Ramos said.

"When?" Dante asked.

"Soon. A day from now, maybe. We'll need to tell the other tribes, and King Yxx of the minotaur.

On the other side of the Bog Lands, Yawl stood in his master's chamber, his head low.

"The human female made it safely back to her people with the metallic box," Yawl said.

"Well?" Ragnok asked.

"Gregor was there with a white wolven I've never seen before, and I think they caught my scent. I had to get out of there." Yawl said.

"So, you failed." Ragnok's hand tightens around the hilt of the sword hanging from his waist.

"I know how it works! The human they call Mac told Gregor all you have to do is hold a small metal stick in your hand and think about where you want to go."

Ragnok nods his head. "We need to get that stick. Tomorrow the centaurs march on Wasatch Village, and if Lonas succeeds, we will again fight alongside the army of Ardeuceus."

"With their help and the libmok's we could wipe the wolven off the face of this planet," Yawl said.

Yawl crossed his arms and stood looking over the balcony down at his legions, sparring, preparing for war, for as far as his eye could see.

CHAPTER 12

MAC AND DANTE WERE AWAKE early, and as Mac looked out the dome, he saw the robed figure of Ramos sitting in the field outside their craft in the early morning sunlight. The hood of his robe covered his face, so all Mac could see were two violet eyes glowing from the shadows and Ramos's dark maw extending from within. "Dante, I think your brother is having issues," Mac said. Dante got to his feet with a yawn and cocked his head to the side.

Mac lowered the ramp, and they walked outside to join him, Kim and Stephanie joining a few moments later after they woke up. Ramos sat cross-legged watching the border to the Bog Lands.

"I almost thought we were finally rid of you!" Dante said.

"Hmmm, you wish," Ramos said.

"The purple eyes are a nice touch," Dante said.

"An unexpected feature of my transformation," Ramos said and nodded.

A woodchuck lay dead on the ground a few feet away. It had been there so long all that remained were some tattered pieces of skin and bones.

"Watch this," Ramos said, waving his right hand toward the skeletal rodent. Violet light emanated from his palm like a party streamer, and the bones formed together as if guided by a thousand tiny hands. The woodchuck suddenly sprang to life, smiling and chittering at them.

"Great trick, do you do anything else?" Dante said and laughed.

"How did you get the Robe of Dragaz away from Inga?" Gregor said.

"I answered her riddle." "What was it?" Dante asked.

"Ask her yourself," Ramos said to his brother.

"Fine, be a smart ass," Dante said.

"You're just in time, Ramos. We're opening the cosmic portal this morning. I'll finally get to see my kids again." Mac said.

"I can't wait to see my daughter," Stephanie said.

"What are you waiting for? We don't have much time left. And I'd suggest you gain aid from your people over there. More than thirty thousand centaur warriors and warlocks are coming here tomorrow morning. They intend to raze one village after another until they take over the continent of Eritria. There are at least thirty thousand centaurs, maybe more, heading our way in another day or two, so we need to get some help." Dante said.

Mac walked back inside to retrieve the cosmic portal. When he emerged from the spacecraft, he placed it on the ground about fifty feet from the ship.

"Looks like you're not wasting any time," Kim said.

"This should have been done days ago, Lieutenant," Mac replied.

Dante looked at the Colonel, who was in human form, and for the first time, Double Head's words echoed inside his mind. What were they risking by allowing the humans into their world? How much did the wolven really know about Mac and his crew's intentions? After all, they were strangers and perhaps their agenda was not altruistic. Dante pulled his father aside as Mac continued to set up the cosmic portal for activation.

"Father, I must speak to you alone," Dante whispered. Gregor nodded, and the two walked away from the party.

With bated breath, the humans waited to see what would happen next as Mac pressed a small black button on the remote control.

"What if the humans mean us harm? Could Double Head have been right? I was there at his final breath, and his warning about them was sincere." Dante asked.

"Double Head was always so suspicious, and that kept him alive for a long time," Gregor said, shaking his head.

But Dante was afraid, perhaps for the first time in his life.

"Double Head was a wise Chief, father. He only wanted the protection of the clans."

Gregor glared at him with hard eyes. "I have never been misled by my visions, Dante. This is the end of it, and I suggest you soften your edge about the humans."

Gregor walked away, leaving his younger son alone, and as Dante watched the portal slowly open, he wondered if his life would be the same after this. The words *untethered reign* echoed in his mind like the chime of a doomsday clock.

Rings of gold light appeared above the metal box, one turning clockwise, the other counterclockwise, and the space within the rings began to grow dark. A second later, they were staring into the timelessness of space as the cosmic portal found its way back to Earth. Comets whooshed by, and planets unknown to Earth scientists appeared in the space-time window until the known solar system came into view. As the people on Eritria stared dumbfounded at the portal, it suddenly stopped at the destination: the underground facility Mac and his team had departed from at the beginning of their journey. The hangar was a welcome sight to the Earth people who had traveled nine light years to encounter a lifetime of adventure in a matter of days.

"This is it. Anyone else care to step nine light-years across space and time?" Mac said, taking his first uncertain step through the cosmic portal to Earth.

For a moment, his mind conjured images of his body sucked through the doorway into an alternate dimension or being hurled into the vacuum of space to drift eternally as a Mac- cicle, but none of that happened, and he was standing on solid ground instead, looking back at his team light years away and just a step behind at the same time.

"Nothing to it," Mac said. He smiled back at them through the tractor-trailer-sized hole between solar systems.

"Colonel MacDonald? Is that you?" A man's voice said. It came from one of the offices about twenty feet from him in an unlit part of the building.

"Yes, who's there?" Mac asked.

A figure emerged from the dark, wearing a black special operations uniform and wearing a Colt .45 sidearm. The man was limping as he walked toward the Colonel, and in the dim lighting of the hangar, Mac could tell that it was Major Tom Harper, the secretary to General Martin. As his features became visible, Mac could clearly see that there had been some kind of skirmish, because before they left Earth for the Zeta star system, Harper had the smooth, young features of a college boy, and now there was a huge red scar spanning from eye to chin on his right side.

"Major, what happened to you?" Mac asked. "Our above-ground base was overrun by eco-terrorists, sir, in a battle that dragged on for three weeks, but we won and shut them down. This scar on my face here was a lucky strike from some guy with a switchblade knife."

"Is the General, OK? Where are my kids?" Mac asked. His heart was burning.

"Your children are fine, and so is Captain Brandt's daughter. They're currently watching cartoons in another lower level of the compound."

"How long have they been here? And cartoons?!" Mac asked. "That's junk food for their brains, Major."

"About eight months sir. And it's all we have right now. Television service has been knocked out for most of the country for about four weeks, and all of our encrypted channels are top secret information. Obviously, we can't show that to the kids. We've been trying to protect them from the worst of this, but our five-year timeline is shrinking down to about an estimated year, maybe."

"Thank God, you got them out. Where did you find them?"

"They were with your sister in downtown Farmington. All I needed to do was track the chip on her cell phone which brought us within three feet of her. It was close, but we got them out of Missouri before a neutron bomb at the Callaway nuclear power station took out most of that state."

"What about my sister, Lorraine?" Mac asked.

"We had to rescue your kids during a firefight in Farmington when political activists clashed with the local government. I was in the helicopter that lifted them out and took a bullet in the ankle, which is what gave me this attractive limp. Your sister was caught in a crossfire between police and the rebels when we were airlifting her. I'm sorry, sir. She died before any of us could do a thing."

"Oh my god. We were gone too long." Mac said.

"Where's General Martin?" Mac asked.

"I texted his phone. Knowing how his driver is, he'll be here in about forty-five minutes or less. Let me take you to your kids."

"One second," Mac said. He ran back over to the cosmic portal and saw his team peering through.

"Stephanie, come on through and get your daughter."

"Skylar's there with you?" Stephanie asked. "The kids are on another level watching cartoons," Mac replied. "Cartoons?"

"Long story, let's just get them and get back through the cosmic portal before it closes unexpectedly," Mac said.

Captain Brandt walked across the doorway as Mac tossed the remote to Kim. "Here, Kim take the remote. If this gate closes for any reason, keep trying to get it back open; this remote will do me no good nine light years from the device."

"Got it," Kim said. Mac and Stephanie followed the Major to an elevator leading down. "I sure hope this thing stays open."

Meanwhile, on the other side of the universe, Mac and Stephanie got into a large freight elevator with Major Harper. As it descended into the lower levels, Mac began to feel the elation of being reunited with the kids. The doors opened to a room decorated with plush leather chairs, extravagant artwork, and a giant seventy-two-inch television. Inside sat Serena and Bobby staring into it.

"Daddy!" Serena yelled. She ran over and jumped into Mac like a tiny freight train.

"Dad!" Bobby said. "You came back for us." Bobby walked over and hugged his father around Serena.

"You two have both grown since I left," Mac said. Tears soaked his eyes as he held Serena and Bobby.

Stephanie reunited with her daughter Skylar, holding her tightly in her arms and crying with joy.

"Aunt Lorraine's dead," Bobby said. Tears streamed down his face. Mac put Serena down, and he could see the sorrow in his son's eyes.

"I know you guys, I was just told, but we're leaving now. You guys have grown so much.

Stephanie, are you ready to go? "Yes, sir," Stephanie said.

"OK, can we leave right now? It's not good here anymore. People have been dying, Dad, a lot of them." Bobby said.

While he was gone, his little boy had grown a year older, and Mac could not help but think once more that his thirteen-year-old son seemed older and wiser than his years.

The elevator doors opened, and General Martin stepped through. He had a patch over his right eye, and he was wearing a black special operations uniform. Mac thought he looked like a superhero straight out of the action comics.

"Mac! You're back. I thought we'd never see you again.
"

"You almost didn't," Mac said.

"I'll bet. You got here just in time, my friend. It's all we can do to maintain this underground bunker."

"So, I heard. What happened to your eye?" Mac asked.

"Some lousy jerk tossed a wrench at my head, and it smashed my eyeball beyond repair." General Martin said. He was shaking his head. "I shot him through his heart to return the favor." General Martin looked closely at Mac's leather attire with a squinting eye but said nothing.

"We lost Jorgenson and Sparling along the way."

"Sorry to hear that, Mac. Losing people is never easy, but you've done well. Actually, I thought you'd ALL die on the way to that planet, and you're lucky to be alive. Let's get the DSEC board of directors and their families off this planet." The General said. Mac nodded and creased his brow.

"I should warn you that the people we met over there on Eritria, our allies, are on the brink of war," Mac asked.

"Colonel, we have three thousand spec Ops snipers, fifty thousand infantry, and enough explosive ordnance to blow everyone in Maine back to the time of our Lord and savior." General Martin said.

"Alright, because we may need it," Mac replied.

"Good to see you again, Mac." "You too, General."

All of them rode the elevator, and as the doors opened, they saw troops incoming with gear and vehicles.

Stephanie pointed out that the cosmic portal had nearly doubled in size since Mac had gone down to get his kids.

"Not sure that's such a good thing," Stephanie said.

"Yeah, it's growing," Mac replied.

"Let's get as many people and vehicles as possible before this portal does something unpredictable." General Martin said.

Mac and Captain Brandt walked across first with the General and their children in tow. Martin's men began filtering through the portal, some driving nuclear cell-powered tanks and armored vehicles.

"Colonel, every one of our vehicles is powered by a nuclear cell that will last another five hundred years. Once we're cut off from earth that's pretty much it for modern technology." General Martin said.

"We have the cosmic portal and could reopen it anytime though, right?" Mac asked.

"Our best scientists have predicted that days from now a massive tsunami is going to rise up and wash away most of the eastern seaboard, and that's just the start of it. The earthquakes out in the earth's oceans have begun to grow larger. Last month we lost the entire country of England to a killer wave." General Martin said. "Oh my, we *did* get back just in time," Stephanie said.

"You're not kidding. I was wondering if we'd ever make it out of here alive."

The three approached Ramos, Dante, Gregor, and Kim, and as they did, General Martin's one good eye widened noticeably. Mac saw it and smirked. As they talked, a bus full of civilians drove through the portal.

"General Martin, this is Gregor, Chief of the Blood Paw wolven, and his sons Dante and Ramos."

"Welcome to Eritria, General. I wish your arrival was under better circumstances." Gregor said.

"Thank you, Chief, and not to worry, sir. My men are highly trained combat soldiers, and we're here to help in any way we can. And please, call me Dick."

Bobby and Serena approached the group with wide eyes.

"You're werewolves?!" Bobby asked. "So cool!"

"Are you a monster?" Serena asked. "Serena!" Mac said.

Dante laughed. "I'm wolven. Pleased to make your acquaintance" Dante said and knelt to look at her and Bobby.

"I'm Serena, and this is my brother, Bobby," Serena said.

"I'm pleased to meet both of you," Dante said.

"We expect the first wave of centaurs early tomorrow morning," Gregor said.

"I'm leaving for Davendale to recruit the minotaur king Yxx. Dante said.

"I've summoned Saki to help me recruit the other wolven chiefs and inform Double Head's tribe that he was killed in combat.

He reached into a bag attached to his hip and withdrew a silent whistle. He blew on it, and moments later, a large multicolored bird resembling an eagle landed next to him. The bird landed standing head and shoulders above any of them and lowered its head for Ramos to climb aboard.

"I'll be back in the morning with help," Ramos said, and they were off into the sky and out of sight.

"That guy is full of surprises," Mac said. "He saved her family from an invasion of army ants one day, and since then, that bird ignores the rest of the world, but whenever he blows that whistle, BOOM, she's right there," Dante said.

"Can my kids stay in the village until this is over, Gregor?" Mac asked.

"Of course. Anyone who is not fighting should be as far away from here as possible." Gregor said.

"I remember the way back to the village, so I can take the kids and the DSEC folks as well. All we need is some camping supplies," Kim said, and she showed him a walkie-talkie she had acquired from the gear and supplies she had encountered.

"If we need you, or you us, just holler. These batteries will last a month." Kim said.

"Alright, Kim. Take care of my kids." Mac said.

Mac kneels to give his kids a hug and kiss. "Dad, we'll be alright. We can do this." Bobby said. He had been quietly listening to the conversation.

"You are definitely your father's son. OK, Kim, you lead them back." Gregor said.

An hour later, Mac had difficulty holding back his tears watching his children and Stephanie's daughter walk into the woods with Kim and the Deep Space Exploration Consortium executive leadership. He stood next to General Martin, maintaining his military bearing.

"General, I'm officially retiring when this is over," Mac said.

Kim was armed with a plasma rifle, and he was hopeful they would meet no danger until they reached Dante's village. Bobby turned around once more and waved to his father as Mac looked on with loving eyes and an aching heart, and then he was gone.

Bivouac tents were set up all along the forest line as the afternoon wore on. The open plains would be the battlefield for this war, the same place Broad Axe and his army had launched their attack three hundred years before.

"Father, it's time for me to leave and seek out Yxx and gain the support of the Minotaur," Dante said.

"Make haste, Dante," Gregor said.

Gregor remained with Mac while his sons were out alerting the tribes and reflected on the last war when, at the darkest hour, they turned the tide and eradicated Asura's father, Broad Axe.

Ramos was soaring high above the forests on his way to Double Head's village. For the rest of the night, they traveled from one village to another and gained the aid of every tribe on the continent. That would be the hardest conversation of any on his quest for alliance.

"We have to talk to Double Head of the Gore Paw, and then we will speak with Terran of the Frost Blight, Nickodemus of the Dark Claw, and Belial of the Arcane Fist tribe."

Dante ran on swift feet to Davendale through the Raag Mountains to speak with their king Yxx. Along the way, he found an abandoned campsite and the remains of Rasp nailed to a tree, crucified by libmok quills. The little mole- man would have only had another three hours to walk before he made it through the narrow pass. Dante hung his head and said a word for his friend, and then he ran on into the night toward Davendale. When he arrived, the forty- foot-tall wood gate was closed, and a sentry had been posted at the top. Dante was greeted by a gruff shout and a crossbow bolt sunk into the ground in front of his feet.

"Who's down there?" The sentry said. Dante could see a rack of horns and a set of dark eyes high above him, but not much else.

"It's Dante, of the Blood Paw. I need to speak with Yxx."

"Yxx is asleep, come back tomorrow." The sentry said.

"I can't wait until then. This is important." Dante said.

The sentry led Dante through darkened cobblestone streets to a large house constructed of carved river stones. The moonlight overhead was their only illumination as they passed by closed shops and the homes of the sleeping minotaur people.

When they arrived at Yxx's house, the sentry knocked on the door, waited a moment, and then produced a key ring, unlocking the door. It creaked open, splitting the silence, and then the sentry stepped out of the way.

"Good luck." He said and stepped out of the way.

Dante walked inside the King's home, his feet creaking loudly on the floorboards. He could hear the king snoring, and then it stopped, and he was standing in the dark, in the minotaur king's house, in silence. A lantern broke the dark as Yxx approached from his chamber.

"My apologies, King Yxx, but Asura's army seeks to claim Eritria, and they march on Wasatch Forest first," Dante said.

"You're sure about this?" Yxx asked. Dante nodded.

"You'll have my army of minotaur's at your side, wolven," Yxx said.

"When can you be ready?"

Yxx walked over to his fireplace, where a large double-bladed battle ax was mounted to the wall, and removed it from the mantle.

"Now," Yxx said.

In two hours, a more relieved and relaxed Dante marched back to the plains with the entire Minotaur army at his side.

"I stood with your father Gregor through many battles when we were young braves, and I would stand beside him to the end of Eritria." "It's good to have your support, King,"

Dante said.

Yxx smiled and patted him on the back, and the two walked side by side, leading fifteen thousand battle-hardened, ax-wielding bulls down the mountain toward battle.

CHAPTER 13

WHEN RAMOS RETURNED THE NEXT morning, the wolven tribes had begun moving into the plains outside Wasatch woods. Yawl had seen this as his forces were clearing the Bog Lands, and what he originally thought was going to be an easy victory over the woodland wolven was fast becoming an all-out war for Eritria. Dante had returned with the Minotaur king Yxx and his army of fearless braves, but as Yawl watched the plains fill with his mortal enemies, his mind obsessed with the cosmic portal. One way or the other, it would be in his hands, or he would be dead.

"Sir, their forces are growing larger." Said a centaur soldier.

"No matter. We'll soon have the cosmic portal, or we'll be dead, sergeant." Yawl replied. His sergeant nodded and looked back to the field of battle.

"Best of luck, sir." "And to you, sergeant."

The undead had begun rising out of the swamp as Yawl's warlocks summoned them from their watery graves. The slime bubbled and gurgled as the bones of wolven, centaur, mole men, and other creatures long dead rose up once more, stinking of grave rot and swamp gas.

On the human front, Mac was concerned about the cosmic portal and its growing size.

"General, I don't know if we should leave this thing open much longer. We could fly a Chinook helicopter through there." Mac said.

"You might be right, Mac," General Martin said.

A flatbed truck carrying atomic warheads rolled through the portal.

"I think we have all we need." General Martin said.

Mac pressed the button on his controller, and a second later, the cosmic portal blinked closed. "I don't trust the cosmic portal, General. It occurred to me that the doorway might open so wide that it could suck our two planets together on some bizarre galactic collision." Mac said. "Blow both of our planets to dust?" The General replied.

"Just a theory, but we should limit our use of that thing. We also need to protect it by splitting the remote and cosmic portal device up. If the centaurs get their hands on both pieces, they'll create all kinds of chaos." Mac said.

"Think they'll come for it?" The General asked.

Mac held up the remote.

"I think they let Stephanie go because they didn't have this and tracked her back here."

The general nodded. "You hide the remote, and I'll hide the comic portal device aboard *The Poseidon*. At least then the two pieces will be in separate places."

"I'm concerned that if the wrong people got their hands on the device, they may be inclined to use it in a manner that is detrimental to our plans," Mac said.

Yawl was looking through his telescope and saw the exchange between Mac and The General.

"Remmy, see the man in the black uniform?" Yawl said and handed the telescope to Remmy, a sergeant in the centaur army.

"You mean the one with the eyepatch?" "Yes. He's our primary target. He's got the controller." Yawl said.

"We got him, sir. I'll inform my men." Yawl stood as a symbol of fierce bravery to his centaur soldiers, his body covered in plate battle armor etched with the skulls of wolven and Minotaur. He would have his long-awaited war with the centaurs' fiercest enemy and, finally, take the wolven lands. As the centaur army emerged from the Bog Lands, the sky burned with early morning light. Warlocks continued to summon the spirits of dead bears, libmok, and centaur undead to fight alongside them. Asura summoned his dragon kin from the Isle of Fire, and swarms of fire-breathing death dealers were swooping through the sky like a blanket threatening to blot out the sun.

The wolven, Minotaur, and human armed forces equally matched the supernatural strength of Asura's vile legions. General Martin winked at Mac as his elite special operations forces readied their weapons. Snipers were positioned along the tree line, aimed and ready as tension grew. Human infantry and artillery aligned behind the wolven, all of them nervous and ready to get the fight underway. A silence swept over the vast plains as the allied armies stood motionless, watching for the enemy.

"Highly trained killers against odd creatures with medieval weapons? This won't take long." General Martin said.

"I wouldn't underestimate anything on this planet, sir," Mac said.

He looked over at the General and winked. A second later, he turned as his body transformed into a wolven. Mac grew two feet taller, assuming his wolven form, grinning as General Martin's good eye widened.

"I've been going through some changes lately myself," Mac said.

"I can see that." The General replied, taking a step back.

At last, the centaurs were in sight. Their horde stomped and snarled, clopping their hooves into the loose dirt, kicking up dust and chunks of earth as they neighed and growled. The undead were among them, taking their unorganized, chaotic formations.

A moment of pre-battle silence sent a hush over the field as a sniper dialed in on a front- line centaur. His trigger finger tightened, and in his over-eager state, he squeezed a bit too hard and then the gun went off. The bullet raced through the air, entering the centaur's head before the report was heard, and the centaur fell dead.

Yawl rode to the front of his line.

Dante gave the order to charge, and as he did, all five tribes of the wolven nation howled a battle cry and ran forward to meet their mortal foe on the battlefield. The centaurs raced toward the wolven. As they did, General Martin's snipers began to pick off centaurs one at a time as they trotted down the plains. The battlefield was set, and chaos ensued as blood spilled in torrents. Screams of agony rang through the air as shouts and howls of defiance and rage returned to the enemy. Yawl ran forward, ever the soldier and brawler, with his sword swinging down into the wolven onslaught, cutting down wolf men left and right.

Minotaur's pushed forward, bashing centaurs, and shambling undead. Within minutes the battlefield was a frenzied cauldron of arms, legs, fists, and iron weapons clashing in a chaotic frenzy. From the northwest, the libmok army joined in the fight, rolling across the fields, and springing to their feet brandishing poison quills.

The human infantry was ill-equipped to deal with their enemy and undereducated about their foes' resourceful weapons. When the first of the libmok army encountered the infantry in hand- to-hand combat, the porcupine men took out a large number of the humans with poison-tipped quills. Eventually, plasma rifles split their ranks, sending the libmok's reeling as the powerful energy weapons shredded their numbers. There were now men atop armored vehicles blasting across the battlefield with plasma cannons, but the army of Yawl continued to press forward. Yawl disappeared into the melee, heading directly for the spacecraft. So far, he had been largely unnoticed by the Wolven and Minotaur forces. He could see the human with the patch over his eye taking the metal case up the ramp and disappearing inside the craft.

General Martin was working as fast as he could to secure the cosmic portal before one of their enemies spotted it and tried to take it from him when he realized he had taken an order from Mac for the first time in their career together. Mac still had the remote control, so the two systems were separate, and even if the centaurs did get the cosmic portal, they would not be able to operate it. As he was coming out of the ship, he felt the sharp tip of a spear pierce his chest, and a second later the General was arching over the head of a large and scary centaur.

"Where is the controller for that device you put aboard the star craft?" Yawl asked with a calm voice.

Dante saw the General skewered on Yawl's trident and ran as fast as possible to help. This caught Mac's attention, who looked with horror as his commander and friend were hanging fifteen feet in the air with a steady stream of blood dripping from his mouth.

"Dick!" Mac yelled. He followed Dante through the hordes of combatants, closing the distance between himself and Yawl.

Dante leaped through the air and landed on Yawl's back with his claws and teeth bared. With a swift strike, he slashed Yawl's back open before the centaur general had time to react and ripped muscles and tendons, causing the other to scream in pain and rage. He dropped the general to the ground with a thud, and as General Martin lay gasping for breath on the maroon-colored grass, smeared with his blood, Mac pulled him away.

"You've got to get...away." General Martin said. He was choking on his blood, and his eyes were fixed and dilated.

"Sir, you're going to make it," Mac growled. "Horrible liar. By the way, that wolf thing is a better look for you." He spoke.

"They want the controller." With a final long sigh, the General died in Mac's arms as the heat of battle raged around them.

The controller, he thought. Where was it? The pocket he'd kept it in was empty, and then he saw it directly under Yawl as he and Dante struggled. Mac left the General on the floor, and with all his power, he jumped through the air and kicked Yawl in the side, knocking him off balance. The three of them went tumbling. While the wolven warriors were distracted fighting Yawl, a small libmok named Toga had snuck aboard the craft and took the cosmic portal without anyone spotting him.

On the way out, he found the controller lying on the ground, and with a sly smile, he picked it up, disappearing into the battle a moment later. He sidestepped the dead and dying, going unnoticed by the larger warriors fighting above his head, and vanished into the Bog Lands without a trace.

Yawl kicked Mac hard in the stomach, knocking him backward as Dante ripped off the faceplate and stabbed Yawl in the right eye with one of his claws. As the centaur leader yelped, Mac got to his feet. While Dante had Yawl on his side, he stomped down on his neck, snapping the bones, and suffocating him. Yawl got up, stumbled around for a minute, holding his neck, and fell dead beside General Martin.

"That did not go well," Mac said.

He was holding his broken ribs as he looked down at his dead friend. The two had not always seen eye to eye on everything, but he would miss General Martin. The general had protected his children, and he didn't know if he'd ever be able to repay the late leader.

"Yawl is dead. We have broken the leadership of the centaur army." Dante said.

"Where's the controller?" Mac asked. He panicked and ran inside the ship. "The cosmic portal is gone, too." Mac began uttering expletives in an intricately woven tapestry.

"This is not good," Dante said. He was shaking his head in sorrow.

"I have a feeling it's on its way back to Moktar right now," Mac said.

"We have to go get it before we're too late," Mac said. His eyes were wide, frantic.

Dante took a large knife out of the sheath at his side and cut Yawl's head off. Then he stuck it on the center spike of Yawl's own trident like a pike and began to walk through the battlefield.

An undead centaur named Eog had seen Yawl die and picked up a discarded plasma rifle, aiming it at Dante. Yxx saw it in his peripheral vision and began to run toward the undead minotaur. Holding his dual-bladed battle in one powerful hand, Yxx closed the distance before the minotaur could fire. Dante turned to see the minotaur king engage the undead minotaur just as their bodies clashed.

Bodies are clashing all around them as the battle rages on, preventing Dante from reaching Yxx in time. Dante dropped the head of Yawl and ran. Yxx and the minotaur are rolling on the ground when a report rings out from the rifle. A blue ball of light passes through Yxx, and in his final act, he rises to his knees, bringing his ax down on Eog, splitting his skull in two. Both fell to the ground, dead.

"Yxx, Nooooooo!" Dante yelled.

Gregor's expression turns to sorrow, and a tear escapes his eye.

"What have I done? These weapons are terrible. I never knew it would be so, so, horrifying." Gregor said.

Dante throws his head back in a long, mournful, cry to the sky.

"The cosmic portal must be destroyed!" Dante growled.

With their attention diverted, no one noticed a centaur galloping across the field of battle with a hand grenade, taken from the cache of weapons the humans brought with them. He pulls the pin and tosses the grenade inside *The Poseidon*. In another minute, an enormous explosion rocks the ground. Pieces of shrapnel ripped through enemy and ally alike, creating a massive fire on the battlefield.

Dante walked back and picked up the trident with Yawl's head atop it. libmok corpses, dead centaurs, his slain wolven brethren, and the ruined bodies of the undead littered the plains as Dante proudly displayed their former leader's head for all to see. Ramos was on the far end of the plains raising fallen soldiers to fight against their own. Centaur undead fought the living ones and ran roughshod over the libmok forces. Ramos's eyes burned with a deep purple flame until all that could be seen beneath his hood was brilliant spectral light. The human snipers worked with Ramos' army and were mopping up the battlefield. When the centaurs saw their general's head on his trident, they lost heart and began to flee.

Dante's fears were confirmed about the destructive power of human technology, Gregor thought.

"Let none leave alive!" Gregor shouted as he and Yxx commanded their troops.

Wolven mages cast barrier spells over the bog lands, trapping the centaurs, and leaving them with no egress point. Snipers began picking the centaurs off like fish in a barrel, while wolven and minotaur warriors broke the rest of their ranks and killed every centaur they found.

The remaining libmok's, cowards by nature, slunk away into the mountains back to their homeland as sniper fire and cannon blasts from the humans knocked them from their feet as they ran.

"Father, the cosmic portal is gone," Dante said.

"Well, we'll have to go get it back, and destroy it before something even more awful happens," Gregor said.

"I'll go, father," Dante said. "Who else is with me?"

"I'm going. We were supposed to come here on a mission of peace. The violence is inescapable." Mac said.

"Lick your wounds later, Colonel; we have more work to do," Dante said.

"It's time to destroy that device," Mac said. "Double Head was right, and I would not listen," Gregor remarked.

"To his last breath, he loved our people, and held no ill will against you, father," Dante said.

"I'm coming, too," Ramos said.

"I'm going as well. To keep you boys out of trouble." Gregor said.

"Captain Brandt, are you joining us?" Mac asked.

"Mac, I'm a doctor, and there's a lot of work to do right here. I'll stay and try to save as many lives as possible." Stephanie said.

"Stephanie, good luck. You guys ready to move out?" Mac asked.

"Let's go. This time, we'll all fly," Ramos said. He blew his whistle, and Saki flew down to greet him. After Ramos explained the situation, she called to her kin, and three more beautiful, silk-fleeced birds arrived to carry them over the Bog Lands.

Toga knew shortcuts through the bog, and it took him less time than most to come out the other side. Once he reached the emptied centaurs citadel, Toga ran up the stairs of Scowl castle to the room where Ragnok awaited his general's return.

"Where is Yawl!" Ragnok barked.

"Sir, he died on the battlefield, but not before distracting the wolven so that I could bring you the cosmic portal."

"All dead, sire," Toga said. He handed the case over to Ragnok and placed the control on top of it.

Where are the rest of my men? I just found out that Lonas was killed by Dante and Double Head! Gregor and his sons will pay for taking everything from me." Ragnok said.

He walked over to the mirror, and after a moment the reflective surface began to shimmer. He could see Asura on the other side, perched on his throne.

"You have the human cosmic portal?" Asura asked.

"Yes, master."

"Then walk through the mirror and hand it to me, my friend." Asura hissed.

Ragnok halted for a moment and placed the cosmic portal device on the floor. He then opened a cabinet next to his mirror and pulled out a burlap sack. Inside the bag was a sphere with an arrowhead sticking out. He placed it on a pedestal and aimed the tip at the doorway.

"Halla soku lindrel." He spoke. The magical incantation poured from his lips like slow, rolling fog, and the arrowhead retracted, waiting for a target.

Ragnok then did as requested and walked through the looking glass, holding the metallic case with pride while the mirror solidified behind him.

"But, what about me?" Toga said. "Take me too!" Silence was his answer.

"What about you? Defend the castle from the wolven." Ragnok sneered. He walked through it, and the mirror solidified.

Toga sat on Ragnok's throne and sulked until Ramos, Dante, Mac, and Gregor came running up the stone staircase with their weapons drawn. Gregor entered the room first, and as he did, the dart from Ragnok's magic ball shot across the room, piercing his heart. The wise mystic uttered a single grunt and fell to the hard stone floor, dead.

"Father!" Dante yelled.

"No!" Ramos cried and fell to his knees. "Bring him back, Ramos!" Dante cried.

He was grief-stricken, looking desperately for a way to undo the effect of Ragnok's deadly arrow.

"What would return to his body is something foul, an abomination," Ramos said. He looked up with tears in his eyes and saw Toga sitting on the throne trying to look innocent.

"Where's Ragnok?" Dante yelled. "Where's the cosmic portal?" Mac asked.

"Gone, long gone. Ragnok walked through the mirror to Asura's castle. He took the device with him." Toga said.

"You stole a device from us that has the power to destroy worlds and gave it to a madman who is bent on controlling this one and all the people on it? Why?" Mac asked.

"Because I was told to." Toga said.

Mac took Dante's crossbow and fired a bolt into Toga's forehead. The little libmok was forced back, and as the bolt entered his skull, it pinned his head to the wooden throne, killing him instantly. Dante sprinkled some of his powder over Gregor's corpse, and they watched him dissolve into dust.

Dante and Ramos gave him a brief look, and Mac shrugged. Ramos wiggled his fingers using his power to reanimate the little libmok. Now undead, but trapped, the small libmok tried in vain to move his head forward and free himself.

"He's not going anywhere for a while," Ramos said.

"Where's Asura's castle?" Mac asked. Dante and Ramos, looking at each other with a pained glance, shook their heads.

"Across the Death Sea, on the Isle of Fire," Dante said.

Ramos looked them each in the eye, and with a snarl in his voice, he said. "Let's go." Meanwhile, on the Isle of Fire, the lizard king Asura meditated in silence over the metallic box. He sensed the device's supernatural nature and grinned wickedly in the dim light. "You are going to help me accomplish so many things."

Asura pressed the button on the controller and closed his eyes. When he opened them, the portal was open. Two concentric rings of light opened to a lush green landscape, billowy white clouds under a sea of blue sky.

"Where are we going?" Ragnok asked. "The planet Telerum. My father and his legions of reptilians need to know the way is clear for their return to Eritria."

Asura and Ragnok, carrying the cosmic portal, stepped through, and then Asura closed it behind him.

Mac, Dante, and Ramos will return in

In the Company of Wolves: Brothers in Arms

www.ingramcontent.com/pod-product-compliance
Lightning Source LLC
Chambersburg PA
CBHW070926260626
47162CB00007B/2804